THE MA[...] W

"This is a very important s[...] explains the author right at the beginning, *"because it shows how all the comings and goings between our own world and the land of Narnia first began."*

In one of the wettest and coldest summers for years, Polly and Digory decide to explore the attic of the old, tall house. Carefully they step over the rafters and creep along the dark corridor that joins their two houses to the empty house beyond. What will they find? Will it be haunted? Perhaps they might even discover a gang of desperate criminals! At any rate, there must be some mystery involved!

It seems something of a let-down when what they stumble upon is the secret workroom of Digory's Uncle Andrew. But when in a wild experiment he makes Polly vanish right out of the world, it is obvious that the dull summer is changing into a strange and totally thrilling adventure.

THE CHRONICLES OF NARNIA
are all available from Collins

In reading order
The Magician's Nephew
The Lion, the Witch and the Wardrobe
The Horse and His Boy
Prince Caspian
The Voyage of the *Dawn Treader*
The Silver Chair
The Last Battle

C. S. LEWIS

The Magician's Nephew

Illustrated by
Pauline Baynes

Collins
An imprint of HarperCollins*Publishers*

This edition published specially for Dealerfield Ltd in 1998
by HarperCollins*Publishers* Ltd

First published in Great Britain by The Bodley Head 1955
First published in Collins paperback 1980

Collins is an imprint of HarperCollins*Publishers* Ltd,
77-85 Fulham Palace Road, Hammersmith, London W6 8JB

1 3 5 7 9 10 8 6 4 2

ISBN 0 583 33772 4

Printed and bound in Great Britain by
Caledonian International Book Manufacturing Ltd, Glasgow

To The Kilmer Family

CONTENTS

CHAPTER ONE

THE WRONG DOOR

THIS is a story about something that happened long ago when your grandfather was a child. It is a very important story because it shows how all the comings and goings between our own world and the land of Narnia first began.

In those days Mr Sherlock Holmes was still living in Baker Street and the Bastables were looking for treasure in the Lewisham Road. In those days, if you were a boy you had to wear a stiff Eton collar every day, and schools were usually nastier than now. But meals were nicer; and as for sweets, I won't tell you how cheap and good they were, because it would only make your mouth water in vain. And in those days there lived in London a girl called Polly Plummer.

She lived in one of a long row of houses which were all joined together. One morning she was out in the back garden when a boy scrambled up from the garden next door and put his face over the wall. Polly was very surprised because up till now there had never been any children in that house, but only Mr Ketterley and Miss Ketterley, a brother and sister, old bachelor and old maid, living together. So she looked up, full of curiosity. The face of the strange boy was very grubby. It could hardly have been grubbier if he had first rubbed his hands in the earth, and then had a good cry, and then dried his face with his hands. As a matter of fact, this was very nearly what he had been doing.

"Hullo," said Polly.

"Hullo," said the boy. "What's your name?"

"Polly," said Polly. "What's yours?"

"Digory," said the boy.

"I say, what a funny name!" said Polly.

"It isn't half so funny as Polly," said Digory.

"Yes it is," said Polly.

"No, it isn't," said Digory.

"At any rate I *do* wash my face," said Polly, "Which is what you need to do; especially after –" and then she stopped. She had been going to say "After you've been blubbing," but she thought that wouldn't be polite.

"Alright, I have then," said Digory in a much louder voice, like a boy who was so miserable that he didn't care who knew he had been crying. "And so would you," he went on, "if you'd lived all your life in the country and had a pony, and a river at the bottom of the garden, and then been brought to live in a beastly Hole like this."

"London isn't a Hole," said Polly indignantly. But the boy was too wound up to take any notice of her, and he went on –

"And if your father was away in India – and you had to come and live with an Aunt and an Uncle who's mad (who would like that?) – and if the reason was that they were looking after your Mother – and if your Mother was ill and was going to – going to – die." Then his face went the wrong sort of shape as it does if you're trying to keep back your tears.

"I didn't know. I'm sorry," said Polly humbly. And then, because she hardly knew what to say, and also to turn Digory's mind to cheerful subjects, she asked:

"Is Mr Ketterley really mad?"

"Well either he's mad," said Digory, "or there's some other mystery. He has a study on the top floor and Aunt Letty says I must never go up there. Well, that looks fishy to begin with. And then there's another thing. Whenever he

tries to say anything to me at meal times – he never even tries to talk to *her* – she always shuts him up. She says, "Don't worry the boy, Andrew" or "I'm sure Digory doesn't want to hear about *that*" or else "Now, Digory, wouldn't you like to go out and play in the garden?"

"What sort of things does he try to say?"

"I don't know. He never gets far enough. But there's more than that. One night – it was last night in fact – as I was going past the foot of the attic-stairs on my way to bed (and I don't much care for going past them either) I'm sure I heard a yell."

"Perhaps he keeps a mad wife shut up there."

"Yes, I've thought of that."

"Or perhaps he's a coiner."

"Or he might have been a pirate, like the man at the beginning of *Treasure Island*, and be always hiding from his old shipmates."

"How exciting!" said Polly, "I never knew your house was so interesting."

"You may think it interesting," said Digory. "But you wouldn't like it if you had to sleep there. How would you like to lie awake listening for Uncle Andrew's step to come creeping along the passage to your room? And he has such awful eyes."

That was how Polly and Digory got to know one another: and as it was just the beginning of the summer holidays and neither of them was going to the sea that year, they met nearly every day.

Their adventures began chiefly because it was one of the wettest and coldest summers there had been for years. That drove them to do indoor things: you might say, indoor exploration. It is wonderful how much exploring you can do with a stump of candle in a big house, or in a row of houses. Polly had discovered long ago that if you opened a certain little door in the box-room attic of her house you would find the cistern and a dark place behind it which you could get into by a little careful climbing. The dark place was like a long tunnel with brick wall on one side and sloping roof on the other. In the roof there were little chunks of light between the slates. There was no floor in this tunnel: you had to step from rafter to rafter, and between them there was only plaster. If you stepped on this you would find yourself falling through the ceiling of the room below. Polly had used the bit of the tunnel just beside the cistern as a smugglers' cave. She had brought up bits of old packing cases and the seats of broken kitchen chairs, and things of that sort, and spread them across from rafter

to rafter so as to make a bit of floor. Here she kept a cash-box containing various treasures, and a story she was writing and usually a few apples. She had often drunk a quiet bottle of ginger-beer in there: the old bottles made it look more like a smugglers' cave.

Digory quite liked the cave (she wouldn't let him see the story) but he was more interested in exploring.

"Look here," he said. "How long does this tunnel go on for? I mean, does it stop where your house ends?"

"No," said Polly. "The walls don't go out to the roof. It goes on. I don't know how far."

"Then we could get the length of the whole row of houses."

"So we could," said Polly, "And oh, I say!"

"What?"

"We could get *into* the other houses."

"Yes, and get taken up for burglars! No thanks."

"Don't be so jolly clever. I was thinking of the house beyond yours."

"What about it?"

"Why, it's the empty one. Daddy says it's always been empty since we came here."

"I suppose we ought to have a look at it then," said Digory. He was a good deal more excited than you'd have thought from the way he spoke. For of course he was thinking, just as you would have been, of all the reasons why the house might have been empty so long. So was Polly. Neither of them said the word "haunted". And both felt that once the thing had been suggested, it would be feeble not to do it.

"Shall we go and try it now?" said Digory.

"Alright," said Polly.

"Don't if you'd rather not," said Digory.

"I'm game if you are," said she.

"How are we to know we're in the next house but one?"

They decided they would have to go out into the box-room and walk across it taking steps as long as the steps from one rafter to the next. That would give them an idea of how many rafters went to a room. Then they would allow about four more for the passage between the two attics in Polly's house, and then the same number for the maid's bedroom as for the box-room. That would give them the length of the house. When they had done that distance twice they would be at the end of Digory's house;

any door they came to after that would let them into an attic of the empty house.

"But I don't expect it's really empty at all," said Digory.

"What do you expect?"

"I expect someone lives there in secret, only coming in and out at night, with a dark lantern. We shall probably discover a gang of desperate criminals and get a reward. It's all rot to say a house would be empty all those years unless there was some mystery."

"Daddy thought it must be the drains," said Polly.

"Pooh! Grown-ups are always thinking of uninteresting explanations," said Digory. Now that they were talking by daylight in the attic instead of by candlelight in the Smugglers' Cave it seemed much less likely that the empty house would be haunted.

When they had measured the attic they had to get a pencil and do a sum. They both got different answers to it at first, and even when they agreed I am not sure they got it right. They were in a hurry to start on the exploration.

"We mustn't make a sound," said Polly as they climbed in again behind the cistern. Because it was such an important occasion they took a candle each (Polly had a good store of them in her cave).

It was very dark and dusty and draughty and they stepped from rafter to rafter without a word except when they whispered to one another, "We're opposite *your* attic now" or "this must be halfway through *our* house". And neither of them stumbled and the candles didn't go out, and at last they came where they could see a little door in the brick wall on their right. There was no bolt or handle on this side of it, of course, for the door had been made for getting in, not for getting out; but there was a catch (as there often is on the inside of a

cupboard door) which they felt sure they would be able to turn.

"Shall I?" said Digory.

"I'm game if you are," said Polly, just as she had said before. Both felt that it was becoming very serious, but neither would draw back. Digory pushed round the catch with some difficultly. The door swung open and the sudden daylight made them blink. Then, with a great shock, they saw that they were looking, not into a deserted attic, but into a furnished room. But it seemed empty enough. It was dead silent. Polly's curiosity got the better of her. She blew out her candle and stepped out into the strange room, making no more noise than a mouse.

It was shaped, of course, like an attic, but furnished as a sitting-room. Every bit of the walls was lined with shelves and every bit of the shelves was full of books. A fire was burning in the grate (you remember that it was a very cold wet summer that year) and in front of the fire-place with its back towards them was a high-backed armchair. Between the chair and Polly, and filling most of the middle of the room, was a big table piled with all sorts of things – printed books, and books of the sort you write in, and ink bottles and pens and sealing-wax and a microscope. But what she noticed first was a bright red wooden tray with a number of rings on it. They were in pairs – a yellow one and a green one together, then a little space, and then another yellow one and another green one. They were no bigger than ordinary rings, and no one could help noticing them because they were so bright. They were the most beautiful shiny little things you can imagine. If Polly had been a very little younger she would have wanted to put one in her mouth.

The room was so quiet that you noticed the ticking of the clock at once. And yet, as she now found, it was not absolutely quiet either. There was a faint – a very, very faint – humming sound. If Hoovers had been invented in those days Polly would have thought it was the sound of a Hoover being worked a long way off – several rooms away and several floors below. But it was a nicer sound than that, a more musical tone: only so faint that you could hardly hear it.

"It's alright; there's no one here," said Polly over her shoulder to Digory. She was speaking above a whisper now. And Digory came out, blinking and looking extremely dirty – as indeed Polly was too.

"This is no good," he said. "It's not an empty house at all. We'd better bunk before anyone comes."

"What do you think those are?" said Polly, pointing at the coloured rings.

"Oh come *on*," said Digory. "The sooner –"

He never finished what he was going to say for at that moment something happened. The high-backed chair in front of the fire moved suddenly and there rose up out of it – like a pantomime demon coming up out of a trapdoor – the alarming form of Uncle Andrew. They were not in the empty house at all; they were in Digory's house and in the forbidden study! Both children said "O-o-oh" and realized their terrible mistake. They felt they ought to have known all along that they hadn't gone nearly far enough.

Uncle Andrew was tall and very thin. He had a long clean-shaven face with a sharply-pointed nose and extremely bright eyes and a great tousled mop of grey hair.

Digory was quite speechless, for Uncle Andrew looked a thousand times more alarming than he had ever looked before. Polly was not so frightened yet; but she soon was. For the very first thing Uncle Andrew did was to walk across to the door of the room, shut it, and turn the key in the lock. Then he turned round, fixed the children with his bright eyes, and smiled, showing all his teeth.

"There!" he said. "Now my fool of a sister can't get at you!"

It was dreadfully unlike anything a grown-up would be expected to do. Polly's heart came into her mouth, and she and Digory started backing towards the little door they had come in by. Uncle Andrew was too quick for them. He got behind them and shut that door too and stood in front of it. Then he rubbed his hands and made his knuckles crack. He had very long, beautifully white, fingers.

"I am delighted to see you," he said. "Two children are just what I wanted."

"Please, Mr Ketterley," said Polly. "It's nearly my dinner time and I've got to go home. Will you let us out, please?"

"Not just yet," said Uncle Andrew. "This is too good an opportunity to miss. I wanted two children. You see, I'm in the middle of a great experiment. I've tried it on a guinea-pig and it seemed to work. But then a guinea-pig can't tell you anything. And you can't explain to it how to come back."

"Look here, Uncle Andrew," said Digory, "it really is dinner time and they'll be looking for us in a moment. You must let us out."

"Must?" said Uncle Andrew.

Digory and Polly glanced at one another. They dared not say anything, but the glances meant "Isn't this dreadful?" and "We must humour him."

"If you let us go for our dinner now," said Polly, "we could come back after dinner."

"Ah, but how do I know that you would?" said Uncle Andrew with a cunning smile. Then he seemed to change his mind.

"Well, well," he said, "if you really must go, I suppose you must. I can't expect two youngsters like you to find it much fun talking to an old buffer like me." He sighed and went on. "You've no idea how lonely I sometimes am. But no matter. Go to your dinner. But I must give you a present before you go. It's not every day that I see a little girl in my dingy old study; especially, if I may say so, such a very attractive young lady as yourself."

Polly began to think he might not really be mad after all.

"Wouldn't you like a ring, my dear?" said Uncle Andrew to Polly.

"Do you mean one of those yellow or green ones?" said Polly. "How lovely!"

"Not a green one," said Uncle Andrew. "I'm afraid I can't give the green ones away. But I'd be delighted to give you any of the yellow ones: with my love. Come and try one on."

Polly had now quite got over her fright and felt sure that the old gentleman was not mad; and there was certainly something strangely attractive about those bright rings. She moved over to the tray.

"Why! I declare," she said. "That humming noise gets louder here. It's almost as if the rings were making it."

"What a funny fancy, my dear," said Uncle Andrew with a laugh. It sounded a very natural laugh, but Digory had seen an eager, almost a greedy, look on his face.

"Polly! Don't be a fool!" he shouted. "Don't touch them."

It was too late. Exactly as he spoke, Polly's hand went out to touch one of the rings. And immediately, without a flash or a noise or a warning of any sort, there was no Polly. Digory and his Uncle were alone in the room.

CHAPTER TWO

DIGORY AND HIS UNCLE

It was so sudden, and so horribly unlike anything that had ever happened to Digory even in a nightmare, that he let out a scream. Instantly Uncle Andrew's hand was over his mouth. "None of that!" he hissed in Digory's ear. "If you start making a noise your Mother'll hear it. And you know what a fright might do to her."

As Digory said afterwards, the horrible meanness of getting at a chap in *that* way, almost made him sick. But of course he didn't scream again.

"That's better," said Uncle Andrew. "Perhaps you couldn't help it. It *is* a shock when you first see someone vanish. Why, it gave even me a turn when the guinea-pig did it the other night."

"Was that when you yelled?" asked Digory.

"Oh, you heard *that*, did you? I hope you haven't been spying on me?"

"No, I haven't," said Digory indignantly. "But what's happened to Polly?"

"Congratulate me, my dear boy," said Uncle Andrew, rubbing his hands. "My experiment has succeeded. The little girl's gone – vanished – right out of the world."

"What have you done to her?"

"Sent her to – well – to another place."

"What *do* you mean?" asked Digory.

Uncle Andrew sat down and said, "Well, I'll tell you all about it. Have you ever heard of old Mrs Lefay?"

"Wasn't she a great-aunt or something?" said Digory.

"Not exactly," said Uncle Andrew. "She was my godmother. That's her, there, on the wall."

Digory looked and saw a faded photograph: it showed the face of an old woman in a bonnet. And he could now remember that he had once seen a photo of the same face in an old drawer, at home, in the country. He had asked his Mother who it was and Mother had not seemed to want to talk about the subject much. It was not at all a nice face, Digory thought, though of course with those early photographs one could never really tell.

"Was there – wasn't there – something wrong about her, Uncle Andrew?" he asked.

"Well," said Uncle Andrew with a chuckle, "it depends what you call *wrong*. People are so narrow-minded. She certainly got very queer in later life. Did very unwise things. That was why they shut her up."

"In an asylum, do you mean?"

"Oh no, no, no," said Uncle Andrew in a shocked voice. "Nothing of that sort. Only in prison."

"I say!" said Digory. "What had she done?"

"Ah, poor woman," said Uncle Andrew. "She had been very unwise. There were a good many different things. We needn't go into all that. She was always very kind to me."

"But look here, what has all this got to do with Polly? I do wish you'd –"

"All in good time, my boy," said Uncle Andrew. "They let old Mrs Lefay out before she died and I was one of the very few people whom she would allow to see her in her last illness. She had got to dislike ordinary, ignorant people, you understand. I do myself. But she and I were interested in the same sort of things. It was only a few days before her death that she told me to go to an old bureau in her house and open a secret drawer and bring her a little box that I would find there. The moment I picked up that box I could tell by the pricking in my fingers that I held some great secret in my hands. She gave it me and made me promise that as soon as she was dead I would burn it, unopened, with certain ceremonies. That promise I did not keep."

"Well, then, it was jolly rotten of you," said Digory.

"Rotten?" said Uncle Andrew with a puzzled look.

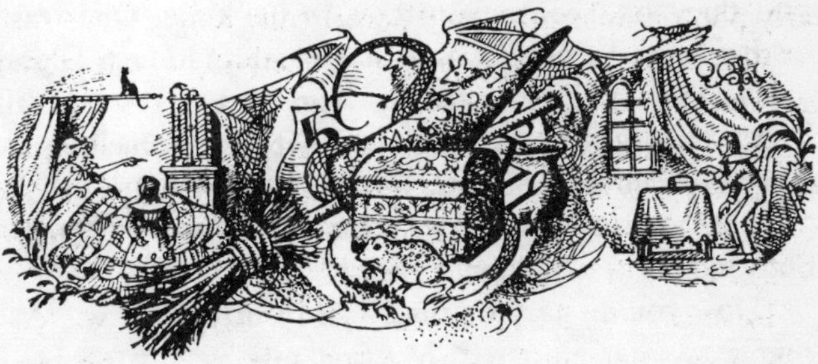

"Oh, I see. You mean that little boys ought to keep their promises. Very true: most right and proper, I'm sure, and I'm very glad you have been taught to do it. But of course you must understand that rules of that sort, however excellent they may be for little boys – and servants – and women – and even people in general, can't possibly be expected to apply to profound students and great thinkers and sages. No, Digory. Men like me, who possess hidden wisdom, are freed from common rules just as we are cut off from common pleasures. Ours, my boy, is a high and lonely destiny."

As he said this he sighed and looked so grave and noble and mysterious that for a second Digory really thought he was saying something rather fine. But then he remembered the ugly look he had seen on his Uncle's face the moment before Polly had vanished: and all at once he saw through Uncle Andrew's grand words. "All it means," he said to himself, "Is that he thinks he can do anything he likes to get anything he wants."

"Of course," said Uncle Andrew, "I didn't dare to open the box for a long time, for I knew it might contain something highly dangerous. For my godmother was a *very* remarkable woman. The truth is, she was one of the last mortals in this country who had fairy blood in her. (She said there had been two others in her time. One was a duchess and the other was a charwoman.) In fact, Digory, you are now talking to the last man (possibly) who really had a fairy godmother. There! That'll be something for you to remember when you are an old man yourself."

"I bet she was a bad fairy," thought Digory; and added out loud. "But what about Polly?"

"How you do harp on that!" said Uncle Andrew. "As if that was what mattered! My first task was of course to study the box itself. It was very ancient. And I knew enough even then to know that it wasn't Greek, or Old Egyptian, or Babylonian, or Hittite, or Chinese. It was older than any of those nations. Ah – that was a great day when I at last found out the truth. The box was Atlantean; it came from the lost island of Atlantis. "That meant it was centuries older than any of the stone-age things they dig up in Europe. And it wasn't a rough, crude thing like them either. For in the very dawn of time Atlantis was already a great city with palaces and temples and learned men."

He paused for a moment as if he expected Digory to say something. But Digory was disliking his Uncle more every minute, so he said nothing.

"Meanwhile," continued Uncle Andrew, "I was learning a good deal in other ways (it wouldn't be proper to explain them to a child) about Magic in general. That meant that I came to have a fair idea what sort of things might be in the box. By various tests I narrowed down the possibilities. I had to get to know some – well, some devilish queer people, and go through some very disagreeable experiences. That was what turned my head grey. One doesn't become a magician for nothing. My health broke down in the end. But I got better. And at last I actually *knew*."

Although there was not really the least chance of anyone overhearing them, he leaned forward and almost whispered as he said:

"The Atlantean box contained something that had been brought from another world when our world was only just beginning."

"What?" asked Digory, who was now interested in spite of himself.

"Only dust," said Uncle Andrew. "Fine, dry dust. Nothing much to look at. Not much to show for a lifetime of toil, you might say. Ah, but when I looked at that dust (I took jolly good care not to touch it) and thought that every grain had once been in another world – I don't mean another planet, you know; they're part of our world and you could get to them if you went far enough – but a really Other World – another Nature – another universe – somewhere you would never reach even if you travelled through the space of this universe for ever and ever – a world that could be reached only by Magic – well!" Here Uncle Andrew rubbed his hands till his knuckles cracked like fireworks.

"I knew," he went on, "that if only you could get it into the right form, that dust would draw you back to the place it had come from. But the difficulty was to get it into the right form. My earlier experiments were all failures. I tried them on guinea-pigs. Some of them only died. Some exploded like little bombs –"

"It was a jolly cruel thing to do," said Digory who had once had a guinea-pig of his own.

"How you do keep getting off the point!" said Uncle Andrew. "That's what the creatures were for. I'd bought them myself. Let me see – where was I? Ah yes. At last I succeeded in making the rings: the yellow rings. But now a new difficulty arose. I was pretty sure, now, that a yellow ring would send any creature that touched it into the Other Place. But what would be the good of that if I couldn't get them back to tell me what they had found there?"

"And what about *them*?" said Digory. "A nice mess they'd be in if they couldn't get back!"

"You will keep on looking at everything from the wrong point of view," said Uncle Andrew with a look of impatience. "Can't you understand that the thing is a great experiment? The whole point of sending anyone into the Other Place is that I want to find out what it's like."

"Well why didn't you go yourself then?"

Digory had hardly ever seen anyone so surprised and offended as his Uncle did at this simple question. "Me? Me?" he exclaimed. "The boy must be mad! A man at my time of life, and in my state of health, to risk the shock and the dangers of being flung suddenly into a different universe? I never heard anything so preposterous in my life! Do you realize what you're saying? Think what Another World means – you might meet anything – anything."

"And I suppose you've sent Polly into it then," said Digory. His cheeks were flaming with anger now. "And all I can say," he added, "even if you are my Uncle – is that you've behaved like a coward, sending a girl to a place you're afraid to go to yourself."

"Silence, sir!" said Uncle Andrew, bringing his hand down on the table. "I will not be talked to like that by a little, dirty, schoolboy. You don't understand. I am the great scholar, the magician, the adept, who is *doing* the experiment. Of course I need subjects to do it *on*. Bless my soul, you'll be telling me next that I ought to have asked the guinea-pigs' permission before I used *them*! No great wisdom can be reached without sacrifice. But the idea of my going myself is ridiculous. It's like asking a general to fight as a common soldier. Supposing I got killed, what would become of my life's work?"

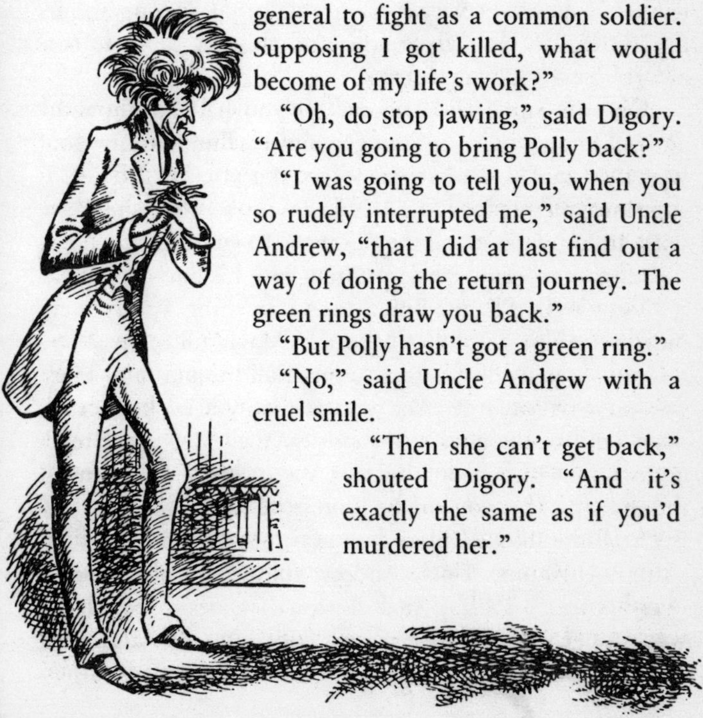

"Oh, do stop jawing," said Digory. "Are you going to bring Polly back?"

"I was going to tell you, when you so rudely interrupted me," said Uncle Andrew, "that I did at last find out a way of doing the return journey. The green rings draw you back."

"But Polly hasn't got a green ring."

"No," said Uncle Andrew with a cruel smile.

"Then she can't get back," shouted Digory. "And it's exactly the same as if you'd murdered her."

"She can get back," said Uncle Andrew, "if someone else will go after her, wearing a yellow ring himself and taking two green rings, one to bring himself back and one to bring her back."

And now of course Digory saw the trap in which he was caught: and he stared at Uncle Andrew, saying nothing, with his mouth wide open. His cheeks had gone very pale.

"I hope," said Uncle Andrew presently in a very high and mighty voice, just as if he were a perfect Uncle who had given one a handsome tip and some good advice, "I *hope*, Digory, you are not given to showing the white feather. I should be very sorry to think that anyone of our family had not enough honour and chivalry to go to the aid of – er – a lady in distress."

"Oh shut up!" said Digory. "If you had any honour and all that, you'd be going yourself. But I know you won't. Alright. I see I've got to go. But you *are* a beast. I suppose you planned the whole thing, so that she'd go without knowing it and then I'd have to go after her."

"Of course," said Uncle Andrew with his hateful smile.

"Very well. I'll go. But there's one thing I jolly well mean to say first. I didn't believe in Magic till today. I see now it's real. Well if it is, I suppose all the old fairy tales are more or less true. And you're simply a wicked, cruel magician like the ones in the stories. Well, I've never read a story in which people of that sort weren't paid out in the end, and I bet you will be. And serve you right."

Of all the things Digory had said this was the first that really went home. Uncle Andrew started and there came over his face a look of such horror that, beast though he was, you could almost feel sorry for him. But a second later he smoothed it all away and said with a rather forced laugh, "Well, well, I suppose that is a natural thing for a child to think – brought up among women, as you have been. Old wives' tales, eh? I don't think you need worry about *my* danger, Digory. Wouldn't it be better to worry about the danger of your little friend? She's been gone some time. If there are any dangers Over There – well, it would be a pity to arrive a moment too late."

"A lot *you* care," said Digory fiercely. "But I'm sick of this jaw. What have I got to do?"

"You really must learn to control that temper of yours, my boy," said Uncle Andrew coolly. "Otherwise you'll grow up like your Aunt Letty. Now. Attend to me."

He got up, put on a pair of gloves, and walked over to the tray that contained the rings.

"They only work," he said, "if they're actually touching your skin. Wearing gloves, I can pick them up – like this – and nothing happens. If you carried one in your pocket nothing would happen: but of course you'd have to be careful not to put your hand in your pocket and touch it by accident. The moment you touch a yellow ring, you vanish out of this world. When you are in the Other Place I expect – of course this hasn't been tested yet, but I *expect* – that the moment you touch a green ring you vanish out of that world and – I expect – reappear in this. Now. I take these two greens and drop them into your right-hand pocket. Remember very carefully which pocket the greens are in. G for green and R for right. G.R. you see: which are the first two letters of green. One for you and one for the little girl. And now you pick up a yellow one for yourself. I should put it on – on your finger – if I were you. There'll be less chance of dropping it."

Digory had almost picked up the yellow ring when he suddenly checked himself.

"Look here," he said. "What about Mother? Supposing she asks where I am?"

"The sooner you go, the sooner you'll be back," said Uncle Andrew cheerfully.

"But you don't really know whether I can get back."

Uncle Andrew shrugged his shoulders, walked across to the door, unlocked it, threw it open, and said:

"Oh very well then. Just as you please. Go down and have your dinner. Leave the little girl to be eaten by wild animals or drowned or starved in Otherworld or lost there for good, if that's what you prefer. It's all one to me. Perhaps before tea time you'd better drop in on Mrs Plummer and explain that she'll never see her daughter again; because you were afraid to put on a ring."

"By gum," said Digory, "don't I just wish I was big enough to punch your head!"

Then he buttoned up his coat, took a deep breath, and picked up the ring. And he thought then, as he always thought afterwards too, that he could not decently have done anything else.

CHAPTER THREE

THE WOOD BETWEEN THE WORLDS

UNCLE ANDREW and his study vanished instantly. Then, for a moment, everything became muddled. The next thing Digory knew was that there was a soft green light coming down on him from above, and darkness below. He didn't seem to be standing on anything, or sitting, or lying. Nothing appeared to be touching him. "I believe I'm in water," said Digory. "Or *under* water." This frightened him for a second, but almost at once he could feel that he was rushing upwards. Then his head suddenly came out into the air and he found himself scrambling ashore, out on to smooth grassy ground at the edge of a pool.

As he rose to his feet he noticed that he was neither dripping nor panting for breath as anyone would expect after being under water. His clothes were perfectly dry. He was standing by the edge of a small pool – not more than ten feet from side to side – in a wood. The trees grew close together and were so leafy that he could get no glimpse of the sky. All the light was green light that came through the leaves: but there must have been a very strong sun overhead, for this green daylight was bright and warm. It was the quietest wood you could possibly imagine. There were no birds, no insects, no animals, and no wind. You could almost feel the trees growing. The pool he had just got out of was not the only pool. There were dozens of others – a pool every few yards as far as his eyes could reach. You could almost feel the trees drinking the water up with their roots. This wood was very much alive. When he tried to describe it afterwards

Digory always said, "It was a *rich* place: as rich as plumcake."

The strangest thing was that, almost before he had looked about him, Digory had half forgotten how he had come there. At any rate, he was certainly not thinking about Polly, or Uncle Andrew, or even his Mother. He was not in the least frightened, or excited, or curious. If anyone had asked him "Where did you come from?" he would probably have said, "I've always been here." That was what it felt like – as if one had always been in that place and never been bored although nothing had ever happened. As he said long afterwards, "It's not the sort of

place where things happen. The trees go on growing, that's all."

After Digory had looked at the wood for a long time he noticed that there was a girl lying on her back at the foot of a tree a few yards away. Her eyes were nearly shut but not quite, as if she were just between sleeping and waking. So he looked at her for a long time and said nothing. And at last she opened her eyes and looked at him for a long time and she also said nothing. Then she spoke, in a dreamy, contented sort of voice.

"I think I've seen you before," she said.

"I rather think so too," said Digory. "Have you been here long?"

"Oh, always," said the girl. "At least – I don't know – a very long time."

"So have I," said Digory.

"No you haven't, said she. "I've just seen you come up out of that pool."

"Yes, I suppose I did," said Digory with a puzzled air, "I'd forgotten."

Then for quite a long time neither said any more.

"Look here," said the girl presently, "I wonder did we ever really meet before? I had a sort of idea – a sort of picture in my head – of a boy and a girl, like us – living somewhere quite different – and doing all sorts of things. Perhaps it was only a dream."

"I've had that same dream, I think," said Digory. "About a boy and a girl, living next door – and something about crawling among rafters. I remember the girl had a dirty face."

"Aren't you getting it mixed? In my dream it was the boy who had the dirty face."

"I can't remember the boy's face," said Digory:

and then added, "Hullo! What's that?"

"Why! it's a guinea-pig," said the girl. And it was – a fat guinea-pig, nosing about in the grass. But round the middle of the guinea-pig there ran a tape, and, tied on to it by the tape, was a bright yellow ring.

"Look! look," cried Digory, "The ring! And look! You've got one on your finger. And so have I."

The girl now sat up, really interested at last. They stared very hard at one another, trying to remember. And then, at exactly the same moment, she shouted out "Mr Ketterley" and he shouted out "Uncle Andrew", and they knew who they were and began to remember the whole story. After a few minutes hard talking they had got it straight. Digory explained how beastly Uncle Andrew had been.

"What do we do now?" said Polly. "Take the guinea-pig and go home?"

"There's no hurry," said Digory with a huge yawn.

"I think there is," said Polly. "This place is too quiet. It's so – so dreamy. You're almost asleep. If we once give in to it we shall just lie down and drowse for ever and ever."

"It's very nice here," said Digory.

"Yes, it is," said Polly.

"But we've got to get back." She stood up and began to go cautiously towards the guinea-pig. But then she changed her mind.

"We might as well leave the guinea-pig," she said. "It's perfectly happy here, and your uncle will only do something horrid to it if we take it home."

"I bet he would," answered Digory. "Look at the way

he's treated *us*. By the way, how *do* we get home?"

"Go back into the pool, I expect."

They came and stood together at the edge looking down into the smooth water. It was full of the reflection of the green, leafy branches; they made it look very deep.

"We haven't any bathing things," said Polly.

"We shan't need them, silly," said Digory. "We're going in with our clothes on. Don't you remember it didn't wet us on the way up?"

"Can you swim?"

"A bit. Can you?"

"Well – not much."

"I don't think we shall need to swim," said Digory "We want to go *down*, don't we?"

Neither of them much liked the idea of jumping into that pool, but neither said so to the other. They took hands and said "One – Two – Three – Go" and jumped. There was a great splash and of course they closed their eyes. But when they opened them again they found they were still standing, hand in hand, in the green wood, and hardly up to their ankles in water. The pool was apparently only a couple of inches deep. They splashed back on to the dry ground.

"What on earth's gone wrong?" said Polly in a frightened voice; but not quite so frightened as you might expect, because it is hard to feel really frightened in that wood. The place is too peaceful.

"Oh! I know," said Digory, "Of course it won't work. We're still wearing our yellow rings. They're for the outward journey, you know. The green ones take you home. We must change rings. Have you got pockets? Good. Put your yellow ring in your left. I've got two greens. Here's one for you."

They put on their green rings and came back to the pool. But before they tried another jump Digory gave a long "O-o-oh!"

"What's the matter?" said Polly.

"I've just had a really wonderful idea," said Digory. "What are all the other pools?"

"How do you mean?"

"Why, if we can get back to our own world by jumping into *this* pool, mightn't we get somewhere else by jumping into one of the others? Supposing there was a world at the bottom of every pool."

"But I thought we were already in your Uncle Andrew's Other World or Other Place or whatever he called it. Didn't you say –"

"Oh bother Uncle Andrew," interrupted Digory. "I don't believe he knows anything about it. He never had the pluck to come here himself. He only talked of *one* Other World. But suppose there were dozens?"

"You mean, this wood might be only one of them?"

"No, I don't believe this wood is a world at all. I think it's just a sort of in-between place."

Polly looked puzzled. "Don't you see?" said Digory. "No, do listen. Think of our tunnel under the slates at home. It isn't a room in any of the houses. In a way, it isn't really part of any of the houses. But once you're in the tunnel you can go along it and come into any of the houses in the row. Mightn't this wood be the same? – a place that isn't in any of the worlds, but once you've found that place you can get into them all."

"Well, even if you can –" began Polly, but Digory went on as if he hadn't heard her.

"And of course that explains everything," he said. "That's why it is so quiet and sleepy here. Nothing ever happens here. Like at home. It's in the houses that people talk, and do things, and have meals. Nothing goes on in the in-between places, behind the walls and above the ceilings and under the floor, or in our own tunnel. But when you come out of our tunnel you may find yourself in *any* house. I think we can get out of this place into jolly well Anywhere! We don't need to jump back into the same pool we came up by. Or not just yet."

"The Wood between the Worlds," said Polly dreamily. "It sounds rather nice."

"Come on," said Digory. "Which pool shall we try?"

"Look here," said Polly, "I'm not going to try any new pool till we've made sure that we *can* get back by the old one. We're not even sure if it'll work yet."

"Yes," said Digory. "And get caught by Uncle Andrew and have our rings taken away before we've had any fun. No thanks."

"Couldn't we just go part of the way down into our own pool," said Polly. "Just to see if it works. Then if it does, we'll change rings and come up again before we're really back in Mr Ketterley's study."

"Can we go *part* of the way down?"

"Well, it took time coming up. I suppose it'll take a little time going back."

Digory made rather a fuss about agreeing to this, but he had to in the end because Polly absolutely refused to do any exploring in new worlds until she had made sure about getting back to the old one. She was quite as brave as he about some dangers (wasps, for instance) but she was not so interested in finding out things nobody had ever heard of before; for Digory was the sort of person who wants to know everything, and when he grew up he became the famous Professor Kirke who comes into other books.

After a good deal of arguing they agreed to put on their green rings ("Green for safety," said Digory, "so you can't help remembering which is which") and hold hands and jump. But as soon as they seemed to be getting back to Uncle Andrew's study, or even to their own world, Polly was to shout "Change" and they would slip off their greens and put on their yellows. Digory wanted to be the one who shouted "Change" but Polly wouldn't agree.

They put on the green rings, took hands, and once more shouted "One – Two – Three – Go". This time it worked. It is very hard to tell you what it felt like, for everything happened so quickly. At first there were bright lights moving about in a black sky; Digory always thinks these were stars and even swears that he saw Jupiter quite close – close enough to see its moon. But almost at once there were rows and rows of roofs and chimney pots about them, and they could see St Paul's and knew they were looking at London. But you could see through the walls of all the houses. Then they could see Uncle Andrew, very vague and shadowy, but getting clearer and more solid-looking all the time, just as if he were coming into focus. But before he became quite real Polly shouted "Change", and they did change, and our world faded away like a dream, and the green light above grew stronger and stronger, till their heads came out of the pool and they scrambled ashore. And there was the wood all about them, as green and bright and still as ever. The whole thing had taken less than a minute.

"There!" said Digory. "That's alright. Now for the adventure. Any pool will do. Come on. Let's try that one."

"Stop!" said Polly. "Aren't we going to mark *this* pool?"

They stared at each other and turned quite white as they realized the dreadful thing that Digory had just been going to do. For there were any number of pools in the wood, and the pools were all alike and the trees were all alike, so that if they had once left behind the pool that led to our own world without making some sort of landmark, the chances would have been a hundred to one against their ever finding it again.

Digory's hand was shaking as he opened his penknife and cut out a long strip of turf on the bank of the pool. The soil (which smelled nice) was of a rich reddish brown and showed up well against the green. "It's a good thing *one* of us has some sense," said Polly.

"Well don't keep on gassing about it," said Digory. "Come along, I want to see what's in one of the other pools." And Polly gave him a pretty sharp answer and he said something even nastier in reply. The quarrel lasted for several minutes but it would be dull to write it all down. Let us skip on to the moment at which they stood with beating hearts and rather scared faces on the edge of the unknown pool with their yellow rings on and held hands and once more said "One – Two – Three – Go!"

Splash! Once again it hadn't worked. This pool, too, appeared to be only a puddle. Instead of reaching a new world they only got their feet wet and splashed their legs for the second time that morning (if it was a morning: it seems to be always the same time in the Wood between the Worlds).

"Blast and botheration!" exclaimed Digory. "What's gone wrong now? We've put our yellow rings on all right. He said yellow for the outward journey."

Now the truth was that Uncle Andrew, who knew nothing about the Wood between the Worlds, had quite a wrong idea about the rings. The yellow ones weren't "outward" rings and the green ones weren't "homeward" rings; at least, not in the way he thought. The stuff of which both were made had all come from the wood. The stuff in the yellow rings had the power of drawing you into the wood; it was stuff that wanted to get back to its own place, the in-between place. But the stuff in the green rings is stuff that is trying to get out of its own place: so that a green ring would take you out of the wood into a world. Uncle Andrew, you see, was working with things he did not really understand; most magicians are. Of course Digory did not realize the truth quite clearly either, or not till later. But when they had talked it over, they decided to try their green rings on the new pool, just to see what happened.

"I'm game if you are," said Polly. But she really said this because, in her heart of hearts, she now felt sure that neither kind of ring was going to work at all in the new pool, and so there was nothing worse to be afraid of than another splash. I am not quite sure that Digory had not the same feeling. At any rate, when they had both put on their greens and come back to the edge of the water, and taken hands again, they were certainly a good deal more cheerful and less solemn than they had been the first time.

"One – Two – Three – Go!" said Digory. And they jumped.

CHAPTER FOUR

THE BELL AND THE HAMMER

THERE was no doubt about the Magic this time. Down and down they rushed, first through darkness and then through a mass of vague and whirling shapes which might have been almost anything. It grew lighter. Then suddenly they felt that they were standing on something solid. A moment later everything came into focus and they were able to look about them.

"What a queer place!" said Digory.

"I don't like it," said Polly with something like a shudder.

What they noticed first was the light. It wasn't like sunlight, and it wasn't like electric light, or lamps, or candles, or any other light they had ever seen. It was a dull, rather red light, not at all cheerful. It was steady and did not flicker. They were standing on a flat paved surface and buildings rose all around them. There was no roof overhead; they were in a sort of courtyard. The sky was extraordinarily dark – a blue that was almost black. When you had seen that sky you wondered that there should be any light at all.

"It's very funny weather here," said Digory. "I wonder if we've arrived just in time for a thunderstorm; or an eclipse."

"I don't like it," said Polly.

Both of them, without quite knowing why, were talking in whispers. And though there was no reason why they should still go on holding hands after their jump, they didn't let go.

The walls rose very high all round that courtyard. They

had many great windows in them, windows without glass, through which you saw nothing but black darkness. Lower down there were great pillared arches, yawning blackly like the mouths of railway tunnels. It was rather cold.

The stone of which everything was built seemed to be red, but that might only be because of the curious light. It was obviously very old. Many of the flat stones that paved the courtyard had cracks across them. None of them fitted closely together and the sharp corners were all worn off. One of the arched doorways was half filled up with rubble. The two children kept on turning round and round to look at the different sides of the courtyard. One reason was that they were afraid of somebody – or something – looking out of those windows at them when their backs were turned.

"Do you think anyone lives here?" said Digory at last, still in a whisper.

"No," said Polly. "It's all in ruins. We haven't heard a sound since we came."

"Let's stand still and listen for a bit," suggested Digory.

They stood still and listened, but all they could hear was the thump-thump of their own hearts. This place was at least as quiet as the Wood between the Worlds. But it was a different kind of quietness. The silence of the Wood had been rich and warm (you could almost hear the trees growing) and full of life: this was a dead, cold, empty silence. You couldn't imagine anything growing in it.

"Let's go home," said Polly.

"But we haven't seen anything yet," said Digory. "Now we're here, we simply must have a look round."

"I'm sure there's nothing at all interesting here."

"There's not much point in finding a magic ring that

lets you into other worlds if you're afraid to look at them when you've got there."

"Who's talking about being afraid?" said Polly, letting go of Digory's hand.

"I only thought you didn't seem very keen on exploring this place."

"I'll go anywhere you go."

"We can get away the moment we want to," said Digory. "Let's take off our green rings and put them in our right-hand pockets. All we've got to do is to remember that our yellow are in our left-hand pockets. You can keep your hand as near your pocket as you like, but don't put it in or you'll touch your yellow and vanish."

They did this and went quietly up to one of the big arched doorways which led into the inside of the building. And when they stood on the threshold and could look in, they saw it was not so dark inside as they had thought at first. It led into a vast, shadowy hall which appeared to be empty; but on the far side there was a row of pillars with arches between them and through those arches there streamed in some more of the same tired-looking light. They crossed the hall, walking very carefully for fear of holes in the floor or of anything lying about that they might trip over. It seemed a long walk. When they had reached the other side they came out through the arches and found themselves in another and larger courtyard.

"That doesn't look very safe," said Polly, pointing at a place where the wall bulged outward and looked as if it were ready to fall over into the courtyard. In one place a pillar was missing between two arches and the bit that came down to where the top of the pillar ought to have been hung there with nothing to support it. Clearly, the place had been deserted for hundreds, perhaps thousands, of years.

"If it's lasted till now, I suppose it'll last a bit longer," said Digory. "But we must be very quiet. You know a noise sometimes brings things down – like an avalanche in the Alps."

They went on out of that courtyard into another doorway, and up a great flight of steps and through vast rooms that opened out of one another till you were dizzy with the mere size of the place. Every now and then they thought they were going to get out into the open and see what sort of country lay around the enormous palace. But each time they only got into another courtyard. They must have been magnificent places when people were still living there. In one there had once been a fountain. A great stone monster with wide-spread wings stood with its mouth open and you could still see a bit of piping at the back of its mouth, out of which the water used to pour. Under it was a wide stone basin to hold the water; but it was as dry as a bone. In other places there were the dry sticks of some sort of climbing plant which had wound itself round the pillars and helped to pull some of them down. But it had died long ago. And there were no ants or spiders or any of the other living things you expect to see in a ruin; and where the dry earth showed between the broken flagstones there was no grass or moss.

It was all so dreary and all so much the same that even Digory was thinking they had better put on their yellow rings and get back to the warm, green, living forest of the In-between place, when they came to two huge doors of some metal that might possibly be gold. One stood a little ajar. So of course they went to look in. Both started back and drew a long breath: for here at last was something worth seeing.

For a second they thought the room was full of people – hundreds of people, all seated, and all perfectly still. Polly and Digory, as you may guess, stood perfectly still themselves for a good long time, looking in. But presently they decided that what they were looking at could not be real people. There was not a movement nor the sound of

a breath among them all. They were like the most wonderful waxworks you ever saw.

This time Polly took the lead. There was something in this room which interested her more than it interested Digory: all the figures were wearing magnificent clothes. If you were interested in clothes at all, you could hardly help going in to see them closer. And the blaze of their colours made this room look, not exactly cheerful, but at

any rate rich and majestic after all the dust and emptiness of the others. It had more windows, too, and was a good deal lighter.

I can hardly describe the clothes. The figures were all robed and had crowns on their heads. Their robes were of crimson and silvery grey and deep purple and vivid green: and there were patterns, and pictures of flowers and strange beasts, in needlework all over them. Precious stones of astonishing size and brightness stared from their crowns and hung in chains round their necks and peeped out from all the places where anything was fastened.

"Why haven't these clothes all rotted away long ago?" asked Polly.

"Magic," whispered Digory. "Can't you feel it? I bet this whole room is just stiff with enchantments. I could feel it the moment we came in."

"Any one of these dresses would cost hundreds of pounds," said Polly.

But Digory was more interested in the faces, and indeed these were well worth looking at. The people sat in their stone chairs on each side of the room and the floor was left free down the middle. You could walk down and look at the faces in turn.

"They were *nice* people, I think," said Digory.

Polly nodded. All the faces they could see were certainly nice. Both the men and women looked kind and wise, and they seemed to come of a handsome race. But after the children had gone a few steps down the room they came to faces that looked a little different. These were very solemn faces. You felt you would have to mind your P's and Q's, if you ever met living people who looked like that. When they had gone a little further, they found themselves among faces they didn't like: this was about the middle of the room. The faces here looked very strong and proud and happy, but they looked cruel. A little further on they looked crueller. Further on again, they were still cruel but they no longer looked happy. They were even despairing faces: as if the people they belonged to had done dreadful things and also suffered dreadful things. The last figure of all was the most interesting – a woman even more richly dressed than the others, very tall (but every figure in that room was taller than the people of our world), with a look of such fierceness and pride that it took your breath away. Yet she was beautiful too. Years afterwards when he was an old man, Digory said he had never in all his life known a woman so beautiful. It is only fair to add that Polly always said she couldn't see anything specially beautiful about her.

This woman, as I said, was the last: but there were plenty of empty chairs beyond her, as if the room had been intended for a much larger collection of images.

"I do wish we knew the story that's behind all this," said Digory. "Let's go back and look at that table sort of thing in the middle of the room."

The thing in the middle of the room was not exactly a table. It was a square pillar about four feet high and on it there rose a little golden arch from which there hung a little golden bell; and beside this there lay a little golden hammer to hit the bell with.

"I wonder . . . I wonder . . . I wonder . . ." said Digory.

"There seems to be something written here," said Polly, stooping down and looking at the side of the pillar.

"By gum, so there is," said Digory. "But of course we shan't be able to read it."

"Shan't we? I'm not so sure," said Polly.

They both looked at it hard and, as you might have expected, the letters cut in the stone were strange. But now a great wonder happened: for, as they looked, though the shape of the strange letters never altered, they found that they could understand them. If only Digory had remembered what he himself had said a few minutes ago, that this was an enchanted room, he might have guessed that the enchantment was beginning to work. But he was too wild with curiosity to think about that. He was longing more and more to know what was written on the pillar. And very soon they both knew. What it said was something like this – at least this is the sense of it though the poetry, when you read it there, was better:

Make your choice, adventurous Stranger;
Strike the bell and bide the danger,
Or wonder, till it drives you mad,
What would have followed if you had.

"No fear!" said Polly. "We don't want any danger."

"Oh but don't you see it's no good!" said Digory. "We can't get out of it now. We shall always be wondering what else would have happened if we had struck the bell. I'm not going home to be driven mad by always thinking of that. No fear!"

"Don't be so silly," said Polly. "As if anyone would! What does it matter what would have happened?"

"I expect anyone who's come as far as this is bound to go on wondering till it sends him dotty. That's the Magic of it, you see. I can feel it beginning to work on me already."

"Well I don't," said Polly crossly. "And I don't believe you do either. You're just putting it on."

"That's all *you* know," said Digory. "It's because you're a girl. Girls never want to know anything but gossip and rot about people getting engaged."

"You looked exactly like your Uncle when you said that," said Polly.

"Why can't you keep to the point?" said Digory. "What we're talking about is –"

"How exactly like a man!" said Polly in a very grown-up voice; but she added hastily, in her real voice, "And don't say I'm just like a woman, or you'll be a beastly copy-cat."

"I should never dream of calling a kid like you a woman," said Digory loftily.

"Oh, I'm a kid, am I?" said Polly who was now in a

real rage. "Well you needn't be bothered by having a kid with you any longer then. I'm off. I've had enough of this place. And I've had enough of you too – you beastly, stuck-up, obstinate pig!"

"None of that!" said Digory in a voice even nastier than he meant it to be; for he saw Polly's hand moving to her pocket to get hold of her yellow ring. I can't excuse what he did next except by saying that he was very sorry for it afterwards (and so were a good many other people). Before Polly's hand reached her pocket, he grabbed her wrist, leaning across with his back against her chest. Then, keeping her other arm out of the way with his other elbow, he leaned forward, picked up the hammer, and struck the golden bell a light, smart tap. Then he let her go and they fell apart staring at each other and breathing hard. Polly was just beginning to cry, not with fear, and not even because he had hurt her wrist quite badly, but with furious anger. Within two seconds, however, they had something to think about that drove their own quarrels quite out of their minds.

As soon as the bell was struck it gave out a note, a sweet note such as you might have expected, and not very loud. But instead of dying away again, it went on; and as it went on it grew louder. Before a minute had passed it was twice as loud as it had been to begin with. It was soon so loud that if the children had tried to speak (but they weren't thinking of speaking now – they were just standing with their mouths open) they would not have heard one another. Very soon it was so loud that they could not have heard one another even by shouting. And still it grew: all on one note, a continuous sweet sound, though the sweetness had something horrible about it, till all the air in that great room was throbbing with it and they could feel the stone floor trembling under their feet. Then at last it began to be mixed with another sound, a vague, disastrous noise which sounded first like the roar of a distant train, and then like the crash of a falling tree. They heard something like great weights falling. Finally, with a sudden rush and thunder, and a shake that nearly flung them off their feet, about a quarter of the roof at one end of the room fell in, great blocks of masonry fell all round them, and the walls rocked. The noise of the bell stopped. The clouds of dust cleared away. Everything became quiet again.

It was never found out whether the fall of the roof was due to Magic or whether that unbearably loud sound from the bell just happened to strike the note which was more than those crumbling walls could stand.

"There! I hope you're satisfied now," panted Polly.

"Well, it's all over, anyway," said Digory.

And both thought it was; but they had never been more mistaken in their lives.

CHAPTER FIVE

THE DEPLORABLE WORD

THE children were facing one another across the pillar where the bell hung, still trembling, though it no longer gave out any note. Suddenly they heard a soft noise from the end of the room which was still undamaged. They turned quick as lightning to see what it was. One of the robed figures, the furthest-off one of all, the woman whom Digory thought so beautiful, was rising from its chair. When she stood up they realized that she was even taller than they had thought. And you could see at once, not only from her crown and robes, but from the flash of her eyes and the curve of her lips, that she was a great queen. She looked round the room and saw the damage and saw the children, but you could not guess from her face what she thought of either or whether she was surprised. She came forward with long, swift strides.

"Who has awaked me? Who has broken the spell?" she asked.

"I think it must have been me," said Digory.

"You!" said the Queen, laying her hand on his shoulder – a white, beautiful hand, but Digory could feel that it was strong as steel pincers. "You? But you are only a child, a common child. Anyone can see at a glance that you have no drop of royal or noble blood in your veins. How did such as you dare to enter this house?"

"We've come from another world; by Magic," said Polly, who thought it was high time the Queen took some notice of her as well as of Digory.

"Is this true?" said the Queen, still looking at Digory and not giving Polly even a glance.

"Yes, it is," said he.

The Queen put her other hand under his chin and forced it up so that she could see his face better. Digory tried to stare back but he soon had to let his eyes drop. There was something about hers that overpowered him.

After she had studied him for well over a minute, she let go of his chin and said:

"You are no magician. The mark of it is not on you. You must be only the servant of a magician. It is on another's Magic that you have travelled here."

"It was my Uncle Andrew," said Digory.

At the moment, not in the room itself but from somewhere very close, there came, first a rumbling, then a creaking, and then a roar of falling masonry, and floor shook.

"There is great peril here," said the Queen. "The whole palace is breaking up. If we are not out of it in a few minutes we shall be buried under the ruin." She spoke as calmly as if she had been merely mentioning the time of day. "Come," she added, and held out a hand to each of the children. Polly, who was disliking the Queen and feeling rather sulky, would not have let her hand be taken if she could have helped it. But though the Queen spoke so calmly, her movements were as quick as thought. Before Polly knew what was happening her left hand had been caught in a hand so much larger and stronger than her own that she could do nothing about it.

"This is a terrible woman," thought Polly. "She's strong enough to break my arm with one twist. And now that she's got my left hand I can't get at my yellow ring. If I tried to stretch across and get my right hand into my left pocket I mightn't be able to reach it, before she asked me what I was doing. Whatever happens we mustn't let her know about the rings. I do hope Digory has the sense to keep his mouth shut. I wish I could get a word with him alone."

The Queen led them out of the Hall of Images into a long corridor and then through a whole maze of halls and stairs and courtyards. Again and again they heard parts of the great palace collapsing, sometimes quite close to them. Once a huge arch came thundering down only a moment after they had passed through it. The Queen was walking quickly – the children had to trot to keep up with her – but she showed no sign of fear. Digory thought, "She's wonderfully brave. And strong. She's what I call a Queen! I do hope she's going to tell us the story of this place."

She did tell them certain things as they went along: "That is the door to the dungeons," she would say, or "That passage leads to the principal torture chambers," or "This was the old banqueting hall where my great-grandfather bade seven hundred nobles to a feast and killed them all before they had drunk their fill. They had had rebellious thoughts."

They came at last into a hall larger and loftier than any they had yet seen. From its size and from the great doors at the far end, Digory thought that now at last they must be coming to the main entrance. In this he was quite right. The doors were dead black, either ebony or some black metal which is not found in our world. They were fastened with great bars, most of them too high to reach and all too heavy to lift. He wondered how they would get out.

The Queen let go of his hand and raised her arm. She drew herself up to her full height and stood rigid. Then she said something which they couldn't understand (but it sounded horrid) and made an action as if she were throwing something towards the doors. And those high and heavy doors trembled for a second as if they were made of silk and then crumbled away till there was nothing left of them but a heap of dust on the threshold.

"Whew!" whistled Digory.

"Has your master magician, your uncle, power like mine?" asked the Queen, firmly seizing Digory's hand again. "But I shall know later. In the meantime, remember what you have seen. This is what happens to things, and to people, who stand in my way."

Much more light than they had yet seen in that country was pouring in through the now empty doorway, and when the Queen led them out through it they were not

surprised to find themselves in the open air. The wind that blew in their faces was cold, yet somehow stale. They were looking from a high terrace and there was a great landscape out below them.

Low down and near the horizon hung a great, red sun, far bigger than our sun. Digory felt at once that it was also older than ours: a sun near the end of its life, weary of looking down upon that world. To the left of the sun, and higher up, there was a single star, big and bright. Those were the only two things to be seen in the dark sky; they made a dismal group. And on the earth, in every direction, as far as the eye could reach, there spread a vast city in which there was no living thing to be seen. And all the temples, towers, palaces, pyramids, and bridges cast long, disastrous-looking shadows in the light of that withered sun. Once a great river had flowed through the city, but the water had long since vanished, and it was now only a wide ditch of grey dust.

"Look well on that which no eyes will ever see again," said the Queen. "Such was Charn, that great city, the city of the King of Kings, the wonder of the world, perhaps of all worlds. Does your uncle rule any city as great as this, boy?"

"No," said Digory. He was going to explain that Uncle Andrew didn't rule any cities, but the Queen went on:

"It is silent now. But I have stood here when the whole air was full of the noises of Charn; the trampling of feet, the creaking of wheels, the cracking of the whips and the groaning of slaves, the thunder of chariots, and the sacrificial drums beating in the temples. I have stood here (but that was near the end) when the roar of battle went up from every street and the river of Charn ran red." She paused and added, "All in one moment one woman blotted it out for ever."

"Who?" said Digory in a faint voice; but he had already guessed the answer.

"I," said the Queen. "I, Jadis the last Queen, but the Queen of the World."

The two children stood silent, shivering in the cold wind.

"It was my sister's fault," said the Queen. "She drove me to it. May the curse of all the Powers rest upon her forever! At any moment I was ready to make peace – yes and to spare her life too, if only she would yield me the throne. But she would not. Her pride has destroyed the whole world. Even after the war had begun, there was a solemn promise that neither side would use Magic. But when she broke her promise, what could I do? Fool! As if she did not know that I had more Magic than she! She even knew that I had the secret of the Deplorable Word. Did she think – she was always a weakling – that I would not use it?"

"What was it?" said Digory.

"That was the secret of secrets," said the Queen Jadis. "It had long been known to the great kings of our race that there was a word which, if spoken with the proper ceremonies, would destroy all living things except the one who spoke it. But the ancient kings were weak and soft-hearted and bound themselves and all who should come after them with great oaths never even to seek after the knowledge of that word. But I learned it in a secret place and paid a terrible price to learn it. I did not use it until she forced me to it. I fought to overcome her by every other means. I poured out the blood of my armies like water –"

"Beast!" muttered Polly.

"The last great battle," said the Queen, "raged for three days here in Charn itself. For three days I looked down upon it from this very spot. I did not use my power till the last of my soldiers had fallen, and the accursed woman, my sister, at the head of her rebels was halfway up those great stairs that lead up from the city to the terrace. Then I waited till we were so close that we could see one another's faces. She flashed her horrible, wicked eyes upon me and said, "Victory." "Yes," said I, "Victory, but not yours." Then I spoke the Deplorable Word. A moment later I was the only living thing beneath the sun."

"But the people?" gasped Digory.

"What people, boy?" asked the Queen.

"All the ordinary people," said Polly, "who'd never done you any harm. And the women, and the children, and the animals."

"Don't you understand?" said the Queen (still speaking to Digory). "I was the Queen. They were all *my* people. What else were they there for but to do my will?"

"It was rather hard luck on them, all the same," said he.

"I had forgotten that you are only a common boy. How should you understand reasons of State? You must learn, child, that what would be wrong for you or for any of the common people is not wrong in a great Queen such as I. The weight of the world is on our shoulders. We must be freed from all rules. Ours is a high and lonely destiny."

Digory suddenly remembered that Uncle Andrew had used exactly the same words. But they sounded much grander when Queen Jadis said them; perhaps because Uncle Andrew was not seven feet tall and dazzlingly beautiful.

"And what did you do then?" said Digory.

"I had already cast strong spells on the hall where the images of my ancestors sit. And the force of those spells was that I should sleep among them, like an image myself, and need neither food nor fire, though it were a thousand years, till one came and struck the bell and awoke me."

"Was it the Deplorable Word that made the sun like that?" asked Digory.

"Like what?" said Jadis.

"So big, so red, and so cold."

"It has always been so," said Jadis. "At least, for

hundreds of thousands of years. Have you a different sort of sun in your world?"

"Yes, it's smaller and yellower. And it gives a good deal more heat."

The Queen gave a long drawn "A-a-ah!" And Digory saw on her face that same hungry and greedy look which he had lately seen on Uncle Andrew's. "So," she said, "yours is a younger world."

She paused for a moment to look once more at the deserted city – and if she was sorry for all the evil she had done there, she certainly didn't show it – and then said:

"Now, let us be going. It is cold here at the end of all the ages."

"Going where?" asked both the children.

"Where?" repeated Jadis in surprise. "To your world, of course."

Polly and Digory looked at each other, aghast. Polly had disliked the Queen from the first; and even Digory, now that he had heard the story, felt that he had seen quite as much of her as he wanted. Certainly, she was not at all the sort of person one would like to take home. And if they did like, they didn't know how they could. What they wanted was to get away themselves: but Polly couldn't get at her ring and of course Digory couldn't go without her. Digory got very red in the face and stammered.

"Oh – oh – our world. I d-didn't know you wanted to go there."

"What else were you sent here for if not to fetch me?" asked Jadis.

"I'm sure you wouldn't like our world at all," said Digory. "It's not her sort of place, is it Polly? It's very dull; not worth seeing, really."

"It will soon be worth seeing when I rule it," answered the Queen.

"Oh, but you can't," said Digory. "It's not like that. They wouldn't let you, you know."

The Queen gave a contemptuous smile. "Many great kings," she said, "thought they could stand against the House of Charn. But they all fell, and their very names are forgotten. Foolish boy! Do you think that I, with my beauty and my Magic, will not have your whole world at my feet before a year has passed? Prepare your incantations and take me there at once."

"This is perfectly frightful," said Digory to Polly.

"Perhaps you fear for this Uncle of yours," said Jadis. "But if he honours me duly, he shall keep his life and his throne. I am not coming to fight against *him*. He must be a very great Magician, if he has found how to send you here. Is he King of your whole world or only of part?"

"He isn't King of anywhere," said Digory.

"You are lying," said the Queen. "Does not Magic always go with the royal blood? Who ever heard of common people being Magicians? I can see the truth whether you speak it or not. Your Uncle is the great King and the great Enchanter of your world. And by his art he has seen the shadow of my face, in some magic mirror or some enchanted pool; and for the love of my beauty he has made a potent spell which shook your world to its foundations and sent you across the vast gulf between world and world to ask my favour and to bring me to him. Answer me: is that not how it was?"

"Well, not *exactly*," said Digory.

"Not exactly," shouted Polly. "Why, it's absolute bosh from beginning to end."

"Minions!" cried the Queen, turning in rage upon Polly

and seizing her hair, at the very top of her head where it hurts most. But in so doing she let go of both the children's hands. "Now," shouted Digory; and "Quick!" shouted Polly. They plunged their left hands into their pockets. They did not even need to put the rings on. The moment they touched them, the whole of that dreary world vanished from their eyes. They were rushing upward and a warm green light was growing nearer overhead.

CHAPTER SIX

THE BEGINNING OF UNCLE ANDREW'S TROUBLES

"Let go! Let go!" screamed Polly.

"I'm not touching you!" said Digory.

Then their heads came out of the pool and, once more, the sunny quietness of the Wood between the Worlds was all about them, and it seemed richer and warmer and more peaceful than ever after the staleness and ruin of the place they had just left. I think that, if they had been given the chance, they would again have forgotten who they were and where they came from and would have lain down and enjoyed themselves, half asleep, listening to the growing of the trees. But this time there was something that kept them as wide-awake as possible: for as soon as they had got out on to the grass, they found that they were not alone. The Queen, or the Witch (whichever you like to call her) had come up with them, holding on fast by Polly's hair. That was why Polly had been shouting out "Let go!"

This proved, by the way, another thing about the rings which Uncle Andrew hadn't told Digory because he didn't know it himself. In order to jump from world to world by one of those rings you don't need to be wearing or touching it yourself; it is enough if you are touching someone who is touching it. In that way they work like a magnet; and everyone knows that if you pick up a pin with a magnet, any other pin which is touching the first pin will come too.

Now that you saw her in the wood, Queen Jadis looked different. She was much paler than she had been; so pale that hardly any of her beauty was left. And she was stooped and seemed to be finding it hard to breathe, as if the air of that place stifled her. Neither of the children felt in the least afraid of her now.

"Let go! Let go of my hair," said Polly. "What do you mean by it?"

"Here! Let go of her hair. At once," said Digory.

They both turned and struggled with her. They were stronger than she and in a few seconds they had forced her to let go. She reeled back, panting, and there was a look of terror in her eyes.

"Quick, Digory!" said Polly. "Change rings and into the home pool."

"Help! Help! Mercy!" cried the Witch in a faint voice, staggering after them. "Take me with you. You cannot mean to leave me in this horrible place. It is killing me."

"It's a reason of State," said Polly spitefully. "Like when you killed all those people in your own world. Do be quick, Digory." They had put on their green rings, but Digory said:

"Oh bother! What *are* we to do?" He couldn't help feeling a little sorry for the Queen.

"Oh don't be such an ass," said Polly. "Ten to one she's only shamming. Do come *on*." And then both children plunged into the home pool. "It's a good thing we made that mark," thought Polly. But as they jumped Digory felt that a large cold finger and thumb had caught him by the ear. And as they sank down and the confused shapes of our own world began to appear, the grip of that finger and thumb grew stronger. The Witch was apparently recovering her strength. Digory struggled and kicked, but it was not of the least use. In a moment they found themselves in Uncle Andrew's study; and there was

Uncle Andrew himself, staring at the wonderful creature that Digory had brought back from beyond the world.

And well he might stare. Digory and Polly stared too. There was no doubt that the Witch had got over her faintness; and now that one saw her in our own world, with ordinary things around her, she fairly took one's breath away. In Charn she had been alarming enough: in London, she was terrifying. For one thing, they had not realized till now how very big she was. "Hardly human" was what Digory thought when he looked at her; and he may have been right, for some say there is giantish blood in the royal family of Charn. But even her height was nothing compared with her beauty, her fierceness, and her wildness. She looked ten times more alive than most of the people one meets in London. Uncle Andrew was bowing and rubbing his hands and looking, to tell the truth, extremely frightened. He seemed a little shrimp of a creature beside the Witch. And yet, as Polly said afterwards, there was a sort of likeness between her face and his, something in the expression. It was the look that all wicked Magicians have, the "Mark" which Jadis had said she could not find in Digory's face. One good thing about seeing the two together was that you would never again be afraid of Uncle Andrew, any more than you'd be afraid of a worm after you had met a rattlesnake or afraid of a cow after you had met a mad bull.

"Pooh!" thought Digory to himself. "*Him* a Magician! Not much. Now *she's* the real thing."

Uncle Andrew kept on rubbing his hands and bowing. He was trying to say something very polite, but his mouth had gone all dry so that he could not speak. His "experiment" with the rings, as he called it, was turning out more successful than he liked: for though he had dabbled in Magic for years he had always left all the dangers (as far as one can) to other people. Nothing at all like this had ever happened to him before.

Then Jadis spoke; not very loud, but there was something in her voice that made the whole room quiver.

"Where is the Magician who has called me into this world?"

"Ah – ah – Madam," gasped Uncle Andrew, "I am most honoured – highly gratified – a most unexpected pleasure – if only I had had the opportunity of making any preparations – I – I –"

"Where is the Magician, Fool?" said Jadis.

"I – I am, Madam. I hope you will excuse any – er –

liberty these naughty children may have taken. I assure you, there was no intention –"

"You?" said the Queen in a still more terrible voice. Then, in one stride, she crossed the room, seized a great handful of Uncle Andrew's grey hair and pulled his head

back so that his face looked up into hers. Then she studied his face as she had studied Digory's face in the palace of Charn. He blinked and licked his lips nervously all the time. At last she let him go: so suddenly that he reeled back against the wall.

"I see," she said scornfully, "you are a Magician – of a sort. Stand up, dog, and don't sprawl there as if you were speaking to your equals. How do you come to know Magic? *You* are not of royal blood, I'll swear."

"Well – ah – not perhaps in the strict sense,"

stammered Uncle Andrew. "Not exactly royal, Ma'am. The Ketterleys are, however, a very old family. An old Dorsetshire family, Ma'am."

"Peace," said the Witch. "I see what you are. You are a little, peddling Magician who works by rules and books. There is no real Magic in your blood and heart. Your kind was made an end of in my world a thousand years ago. But here I shall allow you to be my servant."

"I should be most happy – delighted to be of any service – a p-pleasure, I assure you."

"Peace! You talk far too much. Listen to your first task. I see we are in a large city. Procure for me at once a chariot or a flying carpet or a well-trained dragon, or whatever is usual for royal and noble persons in your land. Then bring me to places where I can get clothes and jewels and slaves fit for my rank. Tomorrow I will begin the conquest of the world."

"I – I – I'll go and order a cab at once," gasped Uncle Andrew.

"Stop," said the Witch, just as he reached the door. "Do not dream of treachery. My eyes can see through walls and into the minds of men. They will be on you wherever you go. At the first sign of disobedience I will lay such spells on you that anything you sit down on will feel like red hot iron and whenever you lie in a bed there will be invisible blocks of ice at your feet. Now go."

The old man went out, looking like a dog with its tail between its legs.

The children were now afraid that Jadis would have something to say to them about what had happened in the wood. As it turned out, however, she never mentioned it either then or afterwards. I think (and Digory thinks too) that her mind was of a sort which cannot remember that quiet place at all, and however often you took her there and however long you left her there, she would still know nothing about it. Now that she was left alone with the children, she took no notice of either of them. And that was like her too. In Charn she had taken no notice of Polly (till the very end) because Digory was the one she wanted to make use of. Now that she had Uncle Andrew, she took no notice of Digory. I expect most witches are like that. They are not interested in things or people unless they can use them; they are terribly practical. So there was silence in the room for a minute or two. But you could tell by the way Jadis tapped her foot on the floor that she was growing impatient.

Presently she said, as if to herself, "What is the old fool doing? I should have brought a whip." She stalked out of the room in pursuit of Uncle Andrew without one glance at the children.

"Whew!" said Polly, letting out a long breath of relief. "And now I must get home. It's frightfully late. I shall catch it."

"Well do, do come back as soon as you can," said Digory. "This is simply ghastly, having her here. We must make some sort of plan."

"That's up to your Uncle now," said Polly. "It was he who started all this messing about with Magic."

"All the same, you will come back, won't you? Hang it all, you can't leave me alone in a scrape like this."

"I shall go home by the tunnel," said Polly rather coldly. "That'll be the quickest way. And if you want me to come back, hadn't you better say you're sorry?"

"Sorry?" exclaimed Digory. "Well now, if that isn't just like a girl! What have I done?"

"Oh nothing of course," said Polly sarcastically. "Only nearly screwed my wrist off in that room with all the wax-works, like a cowardly bully. Only struck the bell with the hammer, like a silly idiot. Only turned back in the wood so that she had time to catch hold of you before we jumped into our own pool. That's all."

"Oh," said Digory, very surprised. "Well, alright, I'll say I'm sorry. And I really am sorry about what happened in the waxworks room. There: I've said I'm sorry. And now, do be decent and come back. I shall be in a frightful hole if you don't."

"I don't see what's going to happen to you. It's Mr Ketterley who's going to sit on red hot chairs and have ice in his bed, isn't it?"

"It isn't that sort of thing," said Digory. "What I'm bothered about is Mother. Suppose that creature went into her room. She might frighten her to death."

"Oh, I see," said Polly in rather a different voice. "Alright. We'll call it Pax. I'll come back – if I can. But I must go now." And she crawled through the little door into the tunnel; and that dark place among the rafters which had seemed so exciting and adventurous a few hours ago, seemed quite tame and homely now.

We must now go back to Uncle Andrew. His poor old heart went pit-a-pat as he staggered down the attic stairs and he kept on dabbing at his forehead with a handkerchief. When he reached his bedroom, which was the floor below, he locked himself in. And the very first thing he did was to grope in his wardrobe for a bottle and a wine-glass which he always kept hidden there where Aunt Letty could not find them. He poured himself out a glassful of some nasty, grown-up drink and drank it off at one gulp. Then he drew a deep breath.

"Upon my word," he said to himself. "I'm dreadfully shaken. Most upsetting! And at my time of life!"

He poured out a second glass and drank it too; then he began to change his clothes. You have never seen such clothes, but I can remember them. He put on a very high, shiny, stiff collar of the sort that made you hold your chin up all the time. He put on a white waistcoat with a pattern on it and arranged his gold watch chain across the front. He put on his best frock-coat, the one he kept for weddings and funerals. He got out his best tall hat and polished it up. There was a vase of flowers (put there by Aunt Letty) on his dressing table; he took one and put it in his button-hole. He took a clean handkerchief (a lovely one such as you couldn't buy today) out of the little left-hand drawer and put a few drops of scent on it. He took his eye-glass, with the thick black ribbon, and screwed it into his eye; then he looked at himself in the mirror.

Children have one kind of silliness, as you know, and grown-ups have another kind. At this moment Uncle Andrew was beginning to be silly in a very grown-up way. Now that the Witch was no longer in the same room with him he was quickly forgetting how she had frightened him and thinking more and more of her wonderful beauty. He kept on saying to himself, "A dem fine woman, sir, a dem fine woman. A superb creature." He had also somehow managed to forget that it was the children who had got hold of this "superb creature": he felt as if he himself by his Magic had called her out of unknown worlds.

"Andrew, my boy," he said to himself as he looked in the glass, "you're a devilish well preserved fellow for your age. A distinguished-looking man, sir."

You see, the foolish old man was actually beginning to imagine the Witch would fall in love with him. The two drinks probably had something to do with it, and so had his best clothes. But he was, in any case, as vain as a peacock; that was why he had become a Magician.

He unlocked the door, went downstairs, sent the housemaid out to fetch a hansom (everyone had lots of servants in those days) and looked into the drawing-room. There, as he expected, he found Aunt Letty. She was busily mending a mattress. It lay on the floor near the window and she was kneeling on it.

"Ah, Letitia my dear," said Uncle Andrew, "I – ah – have to go out. Just lend me five pounds or so, there's a good gel." ("Gel" was the way he pronounced girl.)

"No, Andrew dear," said Aunty Letty in her firm, quiet voice, without looking up from her work. "I've told you times without number that I *will not* lend you money."

"Now pray don't be troublesome, my dear gel," said Uncle Andrew. "It's most important. You will put me in a deucedly awkward position if you don't."

"Andrew," said Aunt Letty, looking him straight in the face, "I wonder *you* are not ashamed to ask *me* for money."

There was a long, dull story of a grown-up kind behind these words. All you need to know about it is that Uncle Andrew, what with "managing dear Letty's business matters for her", and never doing any work, and running up large bills for brandy and cigars (which Aunt Letty had paid again and again) had made her a good deal poorer than she had been thirty years ago.

"My dear gel," said Uncle Andrew, "you don't understand. I shall have some quite unexpected expenses today. I have to do a little entertaining. Come now, don't be tiresome."

"And who, pray, are *you* going to entertain, Andrew?" asked Aunt Letty.

"A – a most distinguished visitor has just arrived."

"Distinguished fiddlestick!" said Aunt Letty. "There hasn't been a ring at the bell for the last hour."

At that moment the door was suddenly flung open. Aunt Letty looked round and saw with amazement that an enormous woman, splendidly dressed, with bare arms and flashing eyes, stood in the doorway. It was the Witch.

CHAPTER SEVEN

WHAT HAPPENED AT THE FRONT DOOR

"Now, slave, how long am I to wait for my chariot?" thundered the Witch. Uncle Andrew cowered away from her. Now that she was really present, all the silly thoughts he had had while looking at himself in the glass were oozing out of him. But Aunt Letty at once got up from her knees and came over to the centre of the room.

"And who is this young person, Andrew, may I ask?" said Aunt Letty in icy tones.

"Distinguished foreigner – v-very important p-person," he stammered.

"Rubbish!" said Aunt Letty, and then, turning to the Witch, "Get out of my house this moment, you shameless hussy, or I'll send for the police." She thought the Witch must be someone out of a circus and she did not approve of bare arms.

"What woman is this?" said Jadis. "Down on your knees, minion, before I blast you."

"No strong language in this house *if* you please, young woman," said Aunt Letty.

Instantly, as it seemed to Uncle Andrew, the Queen towered up to an even greater height. Fire flashed from her eyes: she flung out her arm with the same gesture and the same horrible-sounding words that had lately turned the palace-gates of Charn to dust. But nothing happened except that Aunt Letty, thinking that those horrible words were meant to be ordinary English, said:

"I thought as much. The woman is drunk. Drunk! She can't even speak clearly."

It must have been a terrible moment for the Witch

when she suddenly realized that her power of turning people into dust, which had been quite real in her own world, was not going to work in ours. But she did not lose her nerve even for a second. Without wasting a thought on her disappointment, she lunged forward,

caught Aunt Letty round the neck and the knees, raised her high above her head as if she had been no heavier than a doll, and threw her across the room. While Aunt Letty was still hurtling through the air, the housemaid (who was having a beautifully exciting morning) put her head in at the door and said, "If you please, sir, the 'ansom's come."

"Lead on, Slave," said the Witch to Uncle Andrew. He began muttering something about "regrettable violence – must really protest", but at a single glance from Jadis he became speechless. She drove him out of the room and out of the house; and Digory came running down the stairs just in time to see the front door close behind them.

"Jiminy!" he said. "She's loose in London. And with Uncle Andrew. I wonder what on earth is going to happen now."

"Oh, Master Digory," said the housemaid (who was really having a wonderful day), "I think Miss Ketterley's hurt herself somehow." So they both rushed into the drawing-room to find out what had happened.

If Aunt Letty had fallen on bare boards or even on the carpet, I suppose all her bones would have been broken: but by great good luck she had fallen on the mattress. Aunt Letty was a very tough old lady: aunts often were in those days. After she had had some *sal volatile* and sat still for a few minutes, she said there was nothing the matter with her except a few bruises. Very soon she was taking charge of the situation.

"Sarah," she said to the housemaid (who had never had such a day before), "go around to the police station at once and tell them there is a dangerous lunatic at large. I will take Mrs Kirke's lunch up myself." Mrs Kirke was, of course, Digory's mother.

When Mother's lunch had been seen to, Digory and Aunt Letty had their own. After that he did some hard thinking.

The problem was how to get the Witch back to her own world, or at any rate out of ours, as soon as possible. Whatever happened, she must not be allowed to go rampaging about the house. Mother must not see her.

And, if possible, she must not be allowed to go rampaging about London either. Digory had not been in the drawing-room when she tried to "blast" Aunt Letty, but he had seen her "blast" the gates at Charn: so he knew her terrible powers and did not know that she had lost any of them by coming into our world. And he knew she meant to conquer our world. At the present moment, as far as he could see, she might be blasting Buckingham Palace or the Houses of Parliament: and it was almost certain that quite a number of policemen had by now been reduced to little heaps of dust. And there didn't seem to be anything he could do about that. "But the rings seem to work like magnets," thought Digory. "If I can only touch her and then slip on my yellow, we shall both go into the Wood between the Worlds. I wonder will she go all faint again there? Was that something the place does to her, or was it only the shock of being pulled out of her own world? But I suppose I'll have to risk that. And how am I to find the beast? I don't suppose Aunt Letty would let me go out, not unless I said where I was going. And I haven't got more than twopence. I'd need any amount of money for buses and trams if I went looking all over London. Anyway, I haven't the faintest idea where to look. I wonder if Uncle Andrew is still with her."

It seemed in the end that the only thing he could do was to wait and hope that Uncle Andrew and the Witch would come back. If they did, he must rush out and get hold of the Witch and put on his yellow Ring before she had a chance to get into the house. This meant that he must watch the front door like a cat watching a mouse's hole; he dared not leave his post for a moment. So he went into the dining-room and "glued his face" as they say, to the window. It was a bow-window from which you could see the steps up to the front door and see up and down the street, so that no one could reach the front door without your knowing. "I wonder what Polly's doing?" thought Digory.

He wondered about this a good deal as the first slow half-hour ticked on. But you need not wonder, for I am going to tell you. She had got home late for her dinner, with her shoes and stockings very wet. And when they asked her where she had been and what on earth she had been doing, she said she had been out with Digory Kirke. Under further questioning she said she had got her feet wet in a pool of water, and that the pool was in a wood. Asked where the wood was, she said she didn't know. Asked if it was in one of the parks, she said truthfully enough that she supposed it might be a sort of park. From all of this Polly's mother got thc idea that Polly had gone off, without telling anyone, to some part of London she didn't know, and gone into a strange park and amused herself jumping into puddles. As a result she was told that she had been very naughty indeed and that she wouldn't be allowed to play with "that Kirke boy" any more if anything of the sort ever happened again. Then she was given dinner with all the nice parts left out and sent to bed for two solid hours. It was a thing that happened to one quite often in those days.

So while Digory was staring out of the dining-room window, Polly was lying in bed, and both were thinking how terribly slowly the time could go. I think, myself, I would rather have been in Polly's position. She had only to wait for the end of her two hours: but every few minutes Digory would hear a cab or a baker's van or a butcher's boy coming round the corner and think "Here she comes", and then find it wasn't. And in between these false alarms, for what seemed hours and hours, the clock ticked on and one big fly – high up and far out of reach – buzzed against the window. It was one of those houses that get very quiet and dull in the afternoon and always seem to smell of mutton.

During his long watching and waiting one small thing happened which I shall have to mention because something important came of it later on. A lady called with some grapes for Digory's Mother; and as the dining-room door was open, Digory couldn't help overhearing Aunt Letty and the lady as they talked in the hall.

"What lovely grapes!" came Aunt Letty's voice. "I'm sure if anything could do her good these would. But poor, dear little Mabel! I'm afraid it would need fruit from the land of youth to help her now. Nothing in *this* world will do much." Then they both lowered their voices and said a lot more that he could not hear.

If he had heard that bit about the land of youth a few days ago he would have thought Aunt Letty was just talking without meaning anything in particular, the way grown-ups do, and it wouldn't have interested him. He almost thought so now. But suddenly it flashed upon his mind that he now knew (even if Aunt Letty didn't) that there really were other worlds and that he himself had been in one of them. At that rate there might be a real Land of Youth somewhere. There might be almost anything. There might be fruit in some other world that would really cure his mother! And oh, oh – Well, you know how it feels if you begin hoping for something that you want desperately badly; you almost fight against the hope because it is too good to be true; you've been disappointed so often before. That was how Digory felt. But it was no good trying to throttle this hope. It might – really, really, it just might be true. So many odd things had happened already. And he had the magic rings. There must be worlds you could get to through every pool in the wood. He could hunt through them all. And then – *Mother well again*. Everything right again. He forgot all about watching for the Witch. His hand was already going into the pocket where he kept the yellow ring, when all at once he heard a sound of galloping.

"Hullo! What's that?" thought Digory. "Fire-engine? I wonder what house is on fire. Great Scott, it's coming here. Why, it's Her."

I needn't tell you who he meant by *Her*.

First came the hansom. There was no one in the driver's seat. On the roof – not sitting, but standing on the roof – swaying with superb balance as it came at full speed round the corner with one wheel in the air – was Jadis the Queen of Queens and the Terror of Charn. Her teeth were bared, her eyes shone like fire, and her long hair streamed out behind her like a comet's tail. She was flogging the horse without mercy. Its nostrils were wide and red and its sides were spotted with foam. It galloped madly up to the front door, missing the lamp-post by an inch, and then reared up on its hind legs. The hansom crashed into the lamp-post and shattered into several pieces. The Witch, with a magnificent jump, had sprung clear just in time and landed on the horse's back. She settled herself astride and leaned forward, whispering things in its ear. They must have been things meant not to quiet it but to madden it. It was on its hind legs again in a moment, and its neigh was like a scream; it was all hoofs and teeth and eyes and tossing mane. Only a splendid rider could have stayed on its back.

Before Digory had recovered his breath a good many other things began to happen. A second hansom dashed up close behind the first: out of it there jumped a fat man in a frock-coat and a policeman. Then came a third hansom with two more policemen in it. After it, came about twenty people (mostly errand boys) on bicycles, all ringing their bells and letting out cheers and cat-calls. Last of

all came a crowd of people on foot: all very hot with running, but obviously enjoying themselves. Windows shot up in all the houses of that street and a housemaid or a butler appeared at every front door. They wanted to see the fun.

Meanwhile an old gentleman had begun to struggle shakily out of the ruins of the first hansom. Several people rushed forward to help him; but as one pulled him one way and another another, perhaps he would have got out quite as quickly on his own. Digory guessed that the old gentleman must be Uncle Andrew but you couldn't see his face; his tall hat had been bashed down over it.

Digory rushed out and joined the crowd.

"That's the woman, that's the woman," cried the fat

man, pointing at Jadis. "Do your duty, Constable. Hundreds and thousands of pounds' worth she's taken out of my shop. Look at that rope of pearls round her neck. That's mine. And she's given me a black eye too, what's more."

"That she 'as, guv'nor," said one of the crowd. "And as lovely a black eye as I'd wish to see. Beautiful bit of work that must 'ave been. Gor! ain't she strong then!"

"You ought to put a nice raw beefsteak on it, Mister, that's what it wants," said a butcher's boy.

"Now then," said the most important of the policemen, "what's all this 'ere?"

"I tell you she –" began the fat man, when someone else called out:

"Don't let the old cove in the cab get away. 'E put 'er up to it."

The old gentleman, who was certainly Uncle Andrew, had just succeeded in standing up and was rubbing his bruises. "Now then," said the policeman, turning to him, "What's all this?"

"Womfle – pomfy – shomf," came Uncle Andrew's voice from inside the hat.

"None of that now," said the policeman sternly. "You'll find this is no laughing matter. Take that 'at off, see?"

This was more easily said than done. But after Uncle Andrew had struggled in vain with the hat for some time, two other policemen seized it by the brim and forced it off.

"Thank you, thank you," said Uncle Andrew in a faint voice. "Thank you. Dear me, I'm terribly shaken. If some-one could give me a small glass of brandy –"

"Now you attend to me, if you please," said the police-man, taking out a very large note book and a very small pencil. "Are you in charge of that there young woman?"

"Look out!" called several voices, and the policeman jumped a step backwards just in time. The horse had aimed a kick at him which would probably have killed him. Then the Witch wheeled the horse round so that she faced the crowd and its hind-legs were on the footpath. She had a long, bright knife in her hand and had been busily cutting the horse free from the wreck of the hansom.

All this time Digory had been trying to get into a position from which he could touch the Witch. This wasn't at all easy because, on the side nearest to him, there were too many people. And in order to get round to the other side he had to pass between the horse's hoofs and the railings of the "area" that surrounded the house; for the Ketterleys' house had a basement. If you know anything about horses, and especially if you had seen what a state that horse was in at the moment, you will realize that this was a ticklish thing to do. Digory knew lots about horses, but he set his teeth and got ready to make a dash for it as soon as he saw a favourable moment.

A red-faced man in a bowler hat had now shouldered his way to the front of the crowd.

"Hi! P'leeceman," he said, "that's my 'orse what she's sitting on, same as it's my cab what she's made matchwood of."

"One at a time, please, one at a time," said the policeman.

"But there ain't no time," said the Cabby. "I know that 'orse better'n you do. 'Tain't an ordinary 'orse. 'Is father was a hofficer's charger in the cavalry, 'e was. And if the young woman goes on hexcitin' 'im, there'll be murder done. 'Ere, let me get at him."

The policeman was only to glad to have a good reason for standing further away from the horse. The Cabby took a step nearer, looked up at Jadis, and said in a not unkindly voice:

"Now, Missie, let me get at 'is 'ead, and just you get off. You're a Lidy, and you don't want all these roughs going for you, do you? You want to go 'ome and 'ave a nice cup of tea and a lay down quiet like; then you'll feel ever so much better." At the same time he stretched out his hand towards the horse's head with the words, "Steady, Strawberry, old boy. Steady now."

Then for the first time the Witch spoke.

"Dog!" came her cold, clear voice, ringing loud above all the other noises. "Dog, unhand our royal charger. We are the Empress Jadis."

CHAPTER EIGHT

THE FIGHT AT THE LAMP-POST

"Ho! Hempress, are you? We'll see about that," said a voice. Then another voice said, "Three cheers for the Hempress of Colney 'Atch" and quite a number joined in. A flush of colour came into the Witch's face and she bowed ever so slightly. But the cheers died away into roars of laughter and she saw that they had only been making fun of her. A change came over her expression and she changed the knife to her left hand. Then, without warning, she did a thing that was dreadful to see. Lightly, easily, as if it were the most ordinary thing in the world, she stretched up her right arm and wrenched off one of the cross-bars of the lamp-post. If she had lost some magical powers in our world, she had not lost her strength; she could break an iron bar as if it were a stick of barley-sugar. She tossed her new weapon up in the air, caught it again, brandished it, and urged the horse forward.

"Now's my chance," thought Digory. He darted between the horse and the railings and began going forward. If only the brute would stay still for a moment he might catch the Witch's heel. As he rushed, he heard a sickening crash and a thud. The Witch had brought the bar down on the chief policeman's helmet: the man fell like a nine-pin.

"Quick, Digory. This *must* be stopped," said a voice beside him. It was Polly, who had rushed down the moment she was allowed out of bed.

"You *are* a brick," said Digory. "Hold on to me tight. You'll have to manage the ring. Yellow, remember. And don't put it on till I shout."

There was a second crash and another policeman crumpled up. There came an angry roar from the crowd: "Pull her down. Get a few paving-stones. Call out the Military." But most of them were getting as far away as they could. The Cabby, however, obviously the bravest as well as the kindest person present, was keeping close to the horse, dodging this way and that to avoid the bar, but still trying to catch Strawberry's head.

The crowd booed and bellowed again. A stone whistled over Digory's head. Then came the voice of the Witch, clear like a great bell, and sounding as if, for once, she were almost happy.

"Scum! You shall pay dearly for this when I have conquered your world. Not one stone of your city will be left. I will make it as Charn, as Felinda, as Sorlois, as Bramandin."

Digory as last caught her ankle. She kicked back with her heel and hit him in the mouth. In his pain he lost hold. His lip was cut and his mouth full of blood. From somewhere very close by came the voice of Uncle Andrew in a sort of trembling scream. "Madam – my dear young lady – for heaven's sake – compose yourself." Digory made a second grab at her heel, and was again shaken off. More men were knocked down by the iron bar. He made a third grab: caught the heel: held on like grim death, shouting to Polly "Go!" then – Oh, thank goodness. The angry, frightened faces had vanished. The angry, frightened voices were silenced. All except Uncle Andrew's. Close beside Digory in the darkness, it was wailing on "Oh, oh, is this delirium? Is it the end? I can't bear it. It's not fair. I never meant to be a Magician. It's all a misunderstanding. It's all my godmother's fault; I must protest against this.

In my state of health too. A very old Dorsetshire family."

"Bother!" thought Digory. 'We didn't want to bring *him* along. My hat, what a picnic. Are you there, Polly?"

"Yes, I'm here. Don't keep on shoving."

"I'm not," began Digory, but before he could say anything more, their heads came out into the warm, green sunshine of the wood. And as they stepped out of the pool Polly cried out:

"Oh look! We've brought the old horse with us too. *And* Mr Ketterley. *And* the Cabby. This is a pretty kettle of fish!"

As soon as the Witch saw that she was once more in the wood she turned pale and bent down till her face touched the mane of the horse. You could see she felt deadly sick. Uncle Andrew was shivering. But Strawberry, the horse, shook his head, gave a cheerful whinny, and seemed to feel better. He became quiet for the first time since Digory had seen him. His ears, which had been laid flat back on his skull, came into their proper position, and the fire went out of his eyes.

"That's right, old boy," said the Cabby, slapping Strawberry's neck. "That's better. Take it easy."

Strawberry did the most natural thing in the world. Being very thirsty (and no wonder) he walked slowly across to the nearest pool and stepped into it to have a drink. Digory was still holding the Witch's heel and Polly was holding Digory's hand. One of the Cabby's hands was on Strawberry; and Uncle Andrew, still very shaky, had just grabbed on the Cabby's other hand.

"Quick," said Polly, with a look at Digory. "Greens!"

So the horse never got his drink. Instead, the whole party found themselves sinking into darkness. Strawberry neighed; Uncle Andrew whimpered. Digory said, "That was a bit of luck."

There was a short pause. Then Polly said, "Oughtn't we to be nearly there now?"

"We do seem to be somewhere," said Digory. "At least I'm standing on something solid."

"Why, so am I, now that I come to think of it," said Polly. "But why's it so dark? I say, do you think we got into the wrong Pool?"

"Perhaps this *is* Charn," said Digory. "Only we've got back in the middle of the night."

"This is not Charn," came the Witch's voice. "This is an empty world. This is Nothing."

And really it was uncommonly like Nothing. There were no stars. It was so dark that they couldn't see one another at all and it made no difference whether you kept your eyes shut or open. Under their feet there was a cool, flat something which might have been earth, and was certainly not grass or wood. The air was cold and dry and there was no wind.

"My doom has come upon me," said the Witch in a voice of horrible calmness.

"Oh don't say that," babbled Uncle Andrew. "My dear young lady, pray don't say such things. It can't be as bad as that. Ah – Cabman – my good man – you don't happen to have a flask about you? A drop of spirits is just what I need."

"Now then, now then," came the Cabby's voice, a good firm, hardy voice. "Keep cool everyone, that's what I say. No bones broken, anyone? Good. Well there's something to be thankful for straight away, and more than anyone could expect after falling all that way. Now, if we've fallen down some diggings – as it might be for a new station on the Underground – someone will come and get us out presently, see! And if we're dead – which I don't deny it might be – well, you got to remember that worse things 'appen at sea and a chap's got to die sometime. And there ain't nothing to be afraid of if a chap's led a decent life. And if you ask me, I think the best thing we could do to pass the time would be sing a 'ymn."

And he did. He struck up at once a harvest thanksgiving hymn, all about crops being "safely gathered in". It was not very suitable to a place which felt as if nothing had ever grown there since the beginning of time, but it was the one he could remember best. He had a fine voice and the children joined in; it was very cheering. Uncle Andrew and the Witch did not join in.

Towards the end of the hymn Digory felt someone plucking at his elbow and from a general smell of brandy and cigars and good clothes he decided that it must be Uncle Andrew. Uncle Andrew was cautiously pulling him away from the others. When they had gone a little distance, the old man put his mouth so close to Digory's ear that it tickled, and whispered:

"Now, my boy. Slip on your ring. Let's be off."

But the Witch had very good ears. "Fool!" came her voice and she leaped off the horse. "Have you forgotten that I can hear men's thoughts? Let go the boy. If you attempt treachery I will take such vengeance upon you as never was heard of in all worlds from the beginning."

"And," added Digory, "if you think I'm such a mean pig as to go off and leave Polly – and the Cabby – and the horse – in a place like this, you're well mistaken."

"You are a very naughty and impertinent little boy," said Uncle Andrew.

"Hush!" said the Cabby. They all listened.

In the darkness something was happening at last. A voice had begun to sing. It was very far away and Digory found it hard to decide from what direction it was coming. Sometimes it seemed to come from all directions at once. Sometimes he almost thought it was coming out of the earth beneath them. Its lower notes were deep enough to be the voice of the earth herself. There were no words. There was hardly even a tune. But it was, beyond comparison, the most beautiful noise he had ever heard. It was so beautiful he could hardly bear it. The horse seemed to like it too; he gave the sort of whinney a horse would give if, after years of being a cab-horse, it found itself back in the old field where it had played as a foal, and saw someone whom it remembered and loved coming across the field to bring it a lump of sugar.

"Gawd!" said the Cabby. "Ain't it lovely?"

Then two wonders happened at the same moment. One was that the voice was suddenly joined by other voices; more voices than you could possibly count. They were in harmony with it, but far higher up the scale: cold, tingling, silvery voices. The second wonder was that the blackness overhead, all at once, was blazing with stars. They didn't come out gently one by one, as they do on a summer evening. One moment there had been nothing but darkness; next moment a thousand, thousand points of light leaped out – single stars, constellations, and planets, brighter and bigger than any in our world. There were no clouds. The new stars and the new voices began at exactly the same time. If you had seen and heard it, as Digory did, you would have felt quite certain that it was the stars themselves which were singing, and that it was the First Voice, the deep one, which had made them appear and made them sing.

"Glory be!" said the Cabby. "I'd ha' been a better man all my life if I'd known there were things like this."

The Voice on the earth was now louder and more triumphant; but the voices in the sky, after singing loudly with it for a time, began to get fainter. And now something else was happening.

Far away, and down near the horizon, the sky began to turn grey. A light wind, very fresh, began to stir. The sky, in that one place, grew slowly and steadily paler. You could see shapes of hills standing up dark against it. All the time the Voice went on singing.

There was soon light enough for them to see one another's faces. The Cabby and the two children had open mouths and shining eyes; they were drinking in the sound, and they looked as if it reminded them of something. Uncle Andrew's mouth was open too, but not open with joy. He looked more as if his chin had simply dropped away from the rest of his face. His shoulders were stopped and his knees shook. He was not liking the Voice. If he could have got away from it by creeping into a rat's hole, he would have done so. But the Witch looked as if, in a way, she understood the music better than any of them. Her mouth was shut, her lips were pressed together, and her fists were clenched. Ever since the song began she had felt that this whole world was filled with a Magic different from hers and stronger. She hated it. She would have smashed that whole world, or all worlds, to pieces, if it would only stop the singing. The horse stood with its ears well forward, and twitching. Every now and then it snorted and stamped the ground. It no longer looked like a tired old cab-horse; you could now well believe that its father had been in battles.

The eastern sky changed from white to pink and from pink to gold. The Voice rose and rose, till all the air was shaking with it. And just as it swelled to the mightiest and most glorious sound it had yet produced, the sun arose.

Digory had never seen such a sun. The sun above the ruins of Charn had looked older than ours: this looked younger. You could imagine that it laughed for joy as it came up. And as its beams shot across the land the travellers could see for the first time what sort of place they were in. It was a valley through which a broad, swift river wound its way, flowing eastward towards the sun. Southward there were mountains, northward there were lower hills. But it was a valley of mere earth, rock and water; there was not a tree, not a bush, not a blade of grass to be seen. The earth was of many colours: they were fresh, hot and vivid. They made you feel excited; until you saw the Singer himself, and then you forgot everything else.

It was a Lion. Huge, shaggy, and bright, it stood facing the risen sun. Its mouth was wide open in song and it was about three hundred yards away.

"This is a terrible world," said the Witch. "We must fly at once. Prepare the Magic."

"I quite agree with you, Madam," said Uncle Andrew. "A most disagreeable place. Completely uncivilized. If only I were a younger man and had a gun –"

"Garn!" said the Cabby. "You don't think you could shoot '*im*, do you?"

"And who *would*?" said Polly.

"Prepare the Magic, old fool," said Jadis.

"Certainly, Madam," said Uncle Andrew cunningly. "I must have both the children touching me. Put on your homeward ring at once, Digory." He wanted to get away without the Witch.

"Oh, it's *rings*, is it?" cried Jadis. She would have had her hands in Digory's pocket before you could say knife, but Digory grabbed Polly and shouted out:

"Take care. If either of you come half an inch nearer, we two will vanish and you'll be left here for good. Yes: I have a ring in my pocket that will take Polly and me home. And look! My hand is just ready. So keep your distance. I'm sorry about you (he looked at the Cabby) and about the horse, but I can't help that. As for you two (he looked at Uncle Andrew and the Queen), you're both magicians, so you ought to enjoy living together."

"'Old your noise, everyone," said the Cabby. "I want to listen to the moosic."

For the song had now changed.

CHAPTER NINE

THE FOUNDING OF NARNIA

THE Lion was pacing to and fro about that empty land and singing his new song. It was softer and more lilting than the song by which he had called up the stars and the sun; a gentle, rippling music. And as he walked and sang the valley grew green with grass. It spread out from the Lion like a pool. It ran up the sides of the little hills like a wave. In a few minutes it was creeping up the lower slopes of the distant mountains, making that young world every moment softer. The light wind could now be heard ruffling the grass. Soon there were other things besides grass. The higher slopes grew dark with heather. Patches of rougher and more bristling green appeared in the valley. Digory did not know what they were until one began coming up quite close to him. It was a little, spiky thing that threw out dozens of arms and covered these arms with green and grew larger at the rate of about an inch every two seconds. There were dozens of these things all round him now. When they were nearly as tall as himself he saw what they were. "Trees!" he exclaimed.

The nuisance of it, as Polly said afterwards, was that you weren't left in peace to watch it all. Just as Digory said "Trees!" he had to jump because Uncle Andrew had sidled up to him again and was going to pick his pocket. It wouldn't have done Uncle Andrew much good if he had succeeded, for he was aiming at the right-hand pocket because he still thought the green rings were "homeward" rings. But of course Digory didn't want to lose either.

"Stop!" cried the Witch. "Stand back. No, further back. If anyone goes within ten paces of either of the children, I will knock out his brains." She was poising in her hand the iron bar that she had torn off the lamp-post, ready to throw it. Somehow no one doubted that she would be a very good shot.

"So!" she said. "You would steal back to your own world with the boy and leave me here."

Uncle Andrew's temper at last got the better of his fears. "Yes, Ma'am, I would," he said. "Most undoubtedly I would. I should be perfectly in my rights. I have been most shamefully, most abominably treated. I have done my best to show you such civilities as were in my power. And what has been my reward? You have robbed – I must repeat the word – *robbed* a highly respectable jeweller. You have insisted on my entertaining you to an exceedingly expensive, not to say ostentatious, lunch, though I was obliged to pawn my watch and chain in order to do so (and let me tell you, Ma'am, that none of our family have been in the habit of frequenting pawnshops, except my cousin Edward, and he was in the Yeomanry). During that indigestible meal – I'm feeling the worse for it at this very moment – your behaviour and conversation attracted the unfavourable attention of everyone present. I feel I have been publicly disgraced. I shall never be able to show my face in that restaurant again. You have assaulted the police. You have stolen –"

"Oh stow it, Guv'nor, do stow it," said the Cabby. "Watchin' and listenin's the thing at present; not talking."

There was certainly plenty to watch and to listen to. The tree which Digory had noticed was now a full-grown beech whose branches swayed gently above his head. They stood on cool, green grass, sprinkled with daisies and buttercups. A little way off, along the river bank, willows were growing. On the other side tangles of flowering currant, lilac, wild rose, and rhododendron closed them in. The horse was tearing up delicious mouthfuls of new grass.

All this time the Lion's song, and his stately prowl, to and fro, backwards and forwards, was going on. What was rather alarming was that at each turn he came a little nearer. Polly was finding the song more and more interesting because she thought she was beginning to see the connection between the music and the things that were happening. When a line of dark firs sprang up on a ridge about a hundred yards away she felt that they were connected with a series of deep, prolonged notes which the Lion had sung a second before. And when he burst into a rapid series of lighter notes she was not surprised to see primroses suddenly appearing in every direction. Thus, with an unspeakable thrill, she felt quite certain that all the things were coming (as she said) "out of the Lion's head". When you listened to his song you heard the things he was making up: when you looked round you, you saw them. This was so exciting that she had no time to be afraid. But Digory and the Cabby could not help feeling a bit nervous as each turn of the Lion's walk brought him nearer. As for Uncle Andrew, his teeth were chattering, but his knees were shaking so that he could not run away.

Suddenly the Witch stepped boldly out towards the Lion. It was coming on, always singing, with a slow, heavy pace. It was only twelve yards away. She raised her arm and flung the iron bar straight at its head.

Nobody, least of all Jadis, could have missed at that range. The bar struck the Lion fair between the eyes. It glanced off and fell with a thud in the grass. The Lion came on. Its walk was neither slower nor faster than before; you could not tell whether it even knew it had been hit. Though its soft pads made no noise, you could feel the earth shake beneath their weight.

The Witch shrieked and ran: in a few moments she was out of sight among the trees. Uncle Andrew turned to do likewise, tripped over a root, and fell flat on his face in a

little brook that ran down to join the river. The children could not move. They were not even quite sure that they wanted to. The Lion paid no attention to them. Its huge red mouth was open, but open in song not in a snarl. It passed by them so close that they could have touched its mane. They were terribly afraid it would turn and look at them, yet in some queer way they wished it would. But for all the notice it took of them they might just as well have been invisible and unsmellable. When it had passed them and gone a few paces further it turned, passed them again, and continued its march eastward.

Uncle Andrew, coughing and spluttering, picked himself up.

"Now, Digory," he said, "we've got rid of that woman, and the brute of a lion is gone. Give me your hand and put on your ring at once."

"Keep off," said Digory, backing away from him. "Keep clear of him, Polly. Come over here beside me. Now I warn you, Uncle Andrew, don't come one step nearer, we'll just vanish."

"Do what you're told this minute, sir," said Uncle Andrew. "You're an extremely disobedient, ill-behaved little boy."

"No fear," said Digory. "We want to stay and see what happens. I thought you wanted to know about other worlds. Don't you like it now you're here?"

"Like it!" exclaimed Uncle Andrew. "Just look at the state I'm in. And it was my best coat and waistcoat, too." He certainly was a dreadful sight by now: for of course, the more dressed up you were to begin with, the worse you look after you've crawled out of a smashed hanson-cab and fallen into a muddy brook. "I'm not saying," he added, "that this is not a most interesting place. If I were a younger man, now – perhaps I could get some lively young fellow to come here first. One of those big-game hunters. Something might be made of this country. The climate is delightful. I never felt such air. I believe it would have done me good if – if circumstances had been more favourable. If only we'd had a gun."

"Guns be blowed," said the Cabby. "I think I'll go and see if I can give Strawberry a rub down. That horse 'as more sense than some 'umans as I could mention." He walked back to Strawberry and began making the hissing noises that grooms make.

"Do you still think *that* Lion could be killed by a gun?" asked Digory. "He didn't mind the iron bar much."

"With all her faults," said Uncle Andrew, "that's a plucky gel, my boy. It was a spirited thing to do." He rubbed his hands and cracked his knuckles, as if he were once more forgetting how the Witch frightened him whenever she was really there.

"It was a wicked thing to do," said Polly. "What harm had he done her?"

"Hullo! What's that?" said Digory. He had darted forward to examine something only a few yards away. "I say, Polly," he called back. "Do come and look."

Uncle Andrew came with her; not because he wanted to see but because he wanted to keep close to the children – there might be a chance of stealing their rings. But when he saw what Digory was looking at, even he began to take an interest. It was a perfect little model of a lamp-post, about three feet high but lengthening, and thickening in proportion, as they watched it; in fact growing just as the trees had grown.

"It's alive too – I mean, it's lit," said Digory. And so it was; though of course, the brightness of the sun made the little flame in the lantern hard to see unless your shadow fell on it.

"Remarkable, most remarkable," muttered Uncle Andrew. "Even I never dreamt of Magic like this. We're in a world where everything, even a lamp-post, comes to life and grows. Now I wonder what sort of seed a lamp-post grows from?"

"Don't you see?" said Digory. "This is where the bar fell – the bar she tore off the lamp-post at home. It sank into the ground and now it's coming up as a young lamp-post." (But not so very young now; it was as tall as Digory while he said this.)

"That's it! Stupendous, stupendous," said Uncle Andrew, rubbing his hands harder than ever. "Ho, ho! They laughed at my Magic. That fool of a sister of mine thinks I'm a lunatic. I wonder what they'll say now? I have discovered a world where everything is bursting with life and growth. Columbus, now, they talk about Columbus. But what was America to this? The commercial possibilities of this country are unbounded. Bring a few old bits of scrap iron here, bury 'em, and up they come as brand new railway engines, battleships, anything you please. They'll cost nothing, and I can sell 'em at full prices in England. I shall be a millionaire. And then the climate! I feel years younger already. I can run it as a health resort. A good sanatorium here might be worth twenty thousand a year. Of course I shall have to let a few people into the secret. The first thing is to get that brute shot."

"You're just like the Witch," said Polly. "All you think of is killing things."

"And then as regards oneself," Uncle Andrew continued, in a happy dream. "There's no knowing how long I might live if I settled here. And that's a big consideration when a fellow has turned sixty. I shouldn't be surprised if I never grew a day older in this country! Stupendous! The land of youth!"

"Oh!" cried Digory. "The land of youth! Do you think it really is?" For of course he remembered what Aunt Letty had said to the lady who brought the grapes, and that sweet hope rushed back upon him. "Uncle Andrew", he said, "do you think there's anything here that would cure Mother?"

"What are you talking about?" said Uncle Andrew. "This isn't a chemist's shop. But as I was saying –"

"You don't care twopence about her," said Digory savagely. "I thought you might; after all, she's your sister as well as my Mother. Well, no matter. I'm jolly well going to ask the Lion himself if he can help me." And he turned and walked briskly away. Polly waited for a moment and then went after him.

"Here! Stop! Come back! The boy's gone mad," said Uncle Andrew. He followed the children at a cautious distance behind; for he didn't want to get too far away from the green rings or too near the Lion.

In a few minutes Digory came to the edge of the wood and there he stopped. The Lion was singing still. But now the song had once more changed. It was more like what we should call a tune, but it was also far wilder. It made you want to run and jump and climb. It made you want to shout. It made you want to rush at other people and either hug them or fight them. It made Digory hot and red

in the face. It had some effect on Uncle Andrew, for Digory could hear him saying, "A spirited gel, sir. It's a pity about her temper, but a dem fine woman all the same, a dem fine woman." But what the song did to the two humans was nothing compared with what it was doing to the country.

Can you imagine a stretch of grassy land bubbling like water in a pot? For that is really the best description of what was happening. In all directions it was swelling into humps. They were of very different sizes, some no bigger than mole-hills, some as big as wheel-barrows, two the size of cottages. And the humps moved and swelled till they burst, and the crumbled earth poured out of them, and from each hump there came out an animal. The moles came out just as you might see a mole come out in England. The dogs came out, barking the moment their heads were free, and struggling as you've seen them do when they are getting through a narrow hole in a hedge. The stags were the queerest to watch, for of course the antlers came up a long time

before the rest of them, so at first Digory thought they were trees. The frogs, who all came up near the river, went straight into it with a plop-plop and a loud croaking. The panthers, leopards and things of that sort, sat down at once to wash the loose earth off their hind quarters and then stood up against the trees to sharpen their front claws. Showers of birds came out of the trees. Butterflies fluttered. Bees got to work on the flowers as if they hadn't a second to lose. But the greatest moment of all was when the biggest hump broke like a small earthquake and out came the sloping back, the large, wise head, and the four baggy-trousered legs of an elephant. And now you could hardly hear the song of the Lion; there was so much cawing, cooing, crowing, braying, neighing, baying, barking, lowing, bleating, and trumpeting.

But though Digory could no longer hear the Lion, he could see it. It was so big and so bright that he could not take his eyes off it. The other animals did not appear to be afraid of it. Indeed, at that very moment, Digory heard the sound of hoofs from behind; a second later the old cab-horse trotted past him and joined the other beasts. (The air had apparently suited him as well as it had suited Uncle Andrew. He no longer looked like the poor, old slave he had been in London; he was picking up his feet and holding his head erect.) And now, for the first time, the Lion was quite silent. He was going to and fro among the animals. And every now and then he would go up to two of them (always two at a time) and touch their noses with his. He would touch two beavers among all the beavers, two leopards among all the leopards, one stag and one deer among all the deer, and leave the rest. Some sorts of animal he passed over altogether. But the pairs which he had touched instantly left their own kinds and followed him. At last he stood still and all the creatures whom he had touched came and stood in a wide circle around him. The others whom he had not touched began to wander away. Their noises faded gradually into the distance. The chosen beasts who remained were now

utterly silent, all with their eyes fixed intently upon the Lion. The cat-like ones gave an occasional twitch of the tail but otherwise all were still. For the first time that day there was complete silence, except for the noise of running water. Digory's heart beat wildly; he knew something very solemn was going to be done. He had not forgotten about his Mother; but he knew jolly well that, even for her, he couldn't interrupt a thing like this.

The Lion, whose eyes never blinked, stared at the animals as hard as if he was going to burn them up with his mere stare. And gradually a change came over them. The smaller ones – the rabbits, moles and such-like – grew a good deal larger. The very big ones – you noticed it most with the elephants – grew a little smaller. Many animals sat up on their hind legs. Most put their heads on one side as if they were trying very hard to understand. The Lion opened his mouth, but no sound came from it; he was breathing out, a long, warm breath; it seemed to sway all the beasts as the wind sways a line of trees. Far overhead from beyond the veil of blue sky which hid them the stars sang again; a pure, cold, difficult music. Then there came a swift flash like fire (but it burnt nobody) either from the sky or from the Lion itself, and every drop of blood tingled in the children's bodies, and the deepest, wildest voice they had ever heard was saying:

"Narnia, Narnia, Narnia, awake. Love. Think. Speak. Be walking trees. Be talking beasts. Be divine waters."

CHAPTER TEN

THE FIRST JOKE AND OTHER MATTERS

It was of course the Lion's voice. The children had long felt sure that he could speak: yet it was a lovely and terrible shock when he did.

Out of the trees wild people stepped forth, gods and goddesses of the wood; with them came Fauns and Satyrs and Dwarfs. Out of the river rose the river god with his Naiad daughters. And all these and all the beasts and birds in their different voices, low or high or thick or clear, replied:

"Hail, Aslan. We hear and obey. We are awake. We love. We think. We speak. We know."

"But please, we don't know very much yet," said a nosey and snorty kind of voice. And that really did make the children jump, for it was the cab-horse who had spoken.

"Good old Strawberry," said Polly. "I *am* glad he was one of the ones picked out to be a Talking Beast." And the Cabby, who was now standing beside the children, said, "Strike me pink. I always did say that 'oss 'ad a lot of sense, though."

"Creatures, I give you yourselves," said the strong, happy voice of Aslan. "I give to you forever this land of Narnia. I give you the woods, the fruits, the rivers. I give you the stars and I give you myself. The Dumb Beasts whom I have not chosen are yours also. Treat them gently and cherish them but do not go back to their ways lest you cease to be Talking Beasts. For out of them you were taken and into them you can return. Do not so."

"No, Aslan, we won't, we won't," said everyone. But one perky jackdaw added in a loud voice, "No fear!" and everyone else had finished just before he said it so that his words came out quite clear in a dead silence; and perhaps you have found out how awful that can be – say, at a party. The Jackdaw became so embarrassed that it hid its head under its wings as if it was going to sleep. And all the other animals began making various queer noises

which are their ways of laughing and which, of course, no one has ever heard in our world. They tried at first to repress it, but Aslan said:

"Laugh and fear not, creatures. Now that you are no longer dumb and witless, you need not always be grave. For jokes as well as justice come in with speech."

So they all let themselves go. And there was such merriment that the Jackdaw himself plucked up courage again and perched on the cab-horse's head, between its ears, clapping its wings, and said:

"Aslan! Aslan! Have I made the first joke? Will everybody always be told how I made the first joke?"

"No, little friend," said the Lion. "You have not *made* the first joke; you have only *been* the first joke." Then everyone laughed more than ever; but the Jackdaw didn't mind and laughed just as loud till the horse shook its head and the Jackdaw lost its balance and fell off, but remembered its wings (they were still new to it) before it reached the ground.

"And now," said Aslan, "Narnia is established. We must next take thought for keeping it safe. I will call some of you to my council. Come hither to me, you the chief Dwarf, and you the River-god, and you Oak and the He-Owl, and both the Ravens and the Bull-Elephant. We must talk together. For though the world is not five hours old an evil has already entered it."

The creatures he had named came forward and he turned away eastward with them. The others all began talking, saying things like "*What* did he say had entered the world? – A Neevil – What's a Neevil? – No, he didn't say a Neevil, he said a weevil – Well, what's that?"

"Look here," said Digory to Polly, "I've got to go after him – Aslan, I mean, the Lion. I must speak to him."

"Do you think we can?" said Polly. "I wouldn't dare."

"I've got to," said Digory. "It's about Mother. If anyone could give me something that would do her good, it would be him."

"I'll come along with you," said the Cabby. "I liked the looks of '*im*. And I don't reckon these other beasts will go for us. And I want a word with old Strawberry."

So all three of them stepped out boldly – or as boldly as

they could – towards the assembly of animals. The creatures were so busy talking to one another and making friends that they didn't notice the three humans until they were very close; nor did they hear Uncle Andrew, who

was standing trembling in his buttoned boots a good way off and shouting (but by no means at the top of his voice).

"Digory! Come back! Come back at once when you're told. I forbid you to go a step further."

When at last they were right in among the animals, the animals all stopped talking and stared at them.

"Well?" said the He-Beaver at last, "what, in the name of Aslan, are these?"

"Please," began Digory in rather a breathless voice, when a Rabbit said, "They're a kind of large lettuce, that's my belief."

"No, we're not, honestly we're not," said Polly hastily. "We're not at all nice to eat."

"There!" said the Mole. "They can talk. Who ever heard of a talking lettuce?"

"Perhaps they're the Second Joke," suggested the Jackdaw.

A Panther, which had been washing its face, stopped for a moment to say, "Well, if they are, they're nothing like so good as the first one. At least, *I* don't see anything very funny about them." It yawned and went on with its wash.

"Oh, please," said Digory. "I'm in such a hurry. I want to see the Lion."

All this time the Cabby had been trying to catch Strawberry's eye. Now he did. "Now, Strawberry, old boy," he said. "You know me. You ain't going to stand there and say as you don't know me."

"What's the Thing talking about, Horse?" said several voices.

"Well," said Strawberry very slowly, "I don't exactly know, I think most of us don't know much about anything yet. But I've a sort of idea I've seen a thing like this before. I've a feeling I lived somewhere else – or was something else – before Aslan woke us all up a few minutes ago. It's all very muddled. Like a dream. But there were things like these three in the dream."

"What?" said the Cabby. "Not know me? Me what used to bring you a hot mash of an evening when you was out of sorts? Me what rubbed you down proper? Me what never forgot to put your cloth on you if you was standing in the cold? I wouldn't 'ave thought it of you, Strawberry."

"It *does* begin to come back," said the Horse thoughtfully. "Yes. Let me think now, let me think. Yes, you used to tie a horrid black thing behind me and then hit me to make me run, and however far I ran this black thing would always be coming rattle-rattle behind me."

"We 'ad our living to earn, see," said the Cabby. "Yours the same as mine. And if there 'adn't been no work and no whip there'd 'ave been no stable, no hay, no mash, and no oats. For you did get a taste of oats when I could afford 'em, which no one can deny."

"Oats?" said the Horse, pricking up his ears. "Yes, I remember something about that. Yes, I remember more and more. You were always sitting up somewhere behind, and I was always running in front, pulling you and the black thing. I know I did all the work."

"Summer, I grant you," said the Cabby. " 'Ot work for you and a cool seat for me. But what about winter, old boy, when you was keeping yourself warm and I was sitting up there with my feet like ice and my nose fair pinched off me with the wind, and my 'ands that numb I couldn't 'ardly 'old the reins?"

"It was a hard, cruel country," said Strawberry. "There was no grass. All hard stones."

"Too true, mate, too true!" said the Cabby. "A 'ard world it was. I always did say those paving-stones weren't fair on any 'oss. That's Lunn'on, that is. I didn't like it no more than what you did. You were a country 'oss, and I was a country man. Used to sing in the choir, I did, down at 'ome. But there wasn't a living for me there."

"Oh please, please," said Digory. "Could we get on? The Lion's getting further and further away. And I do want to speak to him so dreadfully badly."

"Look 'ere, Strawberry," said the Cabby. "This young gen'leman 'as something on his mind that he wants to talk to the Lion about; 'im you call Aslan. Suppose you was to let 'im ride on your back (which 'e'd take it very kindly) and trot 'im over to where the Lion is. And me and the little girl will be following along."

"Ride?" said Strawberry. "Oh, I remember now. That means sitting on my back. I remember there used to be a little one of you two-leggers who used to do that long ago. He used to have little hard, square lumps of some white stuff that he gave me. They tasted – oh, wonderful, sweeter than grass."

"Ah, that'd be sugar," said the Cabby.

"Please, Strawberry," begged Digory, "do, do let me get up and take me to Aslan."

"Well, I don't mind," said the Horse. "Not for once in a way. Up you get."

"Good old Strawberry," said the Cabby. "'Ere, young 'un, I'll give you a lift." Digory was soon on Strawberry's back, and quite comfortable, for he had ridden bare-back before on his own pony.

"Now, do gee up, Strawberry," he said.

"You don't happen to have a bit of that white stuff about you, I suppose?" said the Horse.

"No. I'm afraid I haven't," said Digory.

"Well, it can't be helped," said Strawberry, and off they went.

At that moment a large Bulldog, who had been sniffing and staring very hard, said:

"Look. Isn't there another of these queer creatures –

over there, beside the river, under the trees?"

Then all the animals looked and saw Uncle Andrew, standing very still among the rhododendrons and hoping he wouldn't be noticed.

"Come on!" said several voices. "Let's go and find out." So, while Strawberry was briskly trotting away with Digory in one direction (and Polly and the Cabby were following on foot) most of the creatures rushed towards Uncle Andrew with roars, barks, grunts, and various noises of cheerful interest.

We must now go back a bit and explain what the whole scene had looked like from Uncle Andrew's point of view. It had not made at all the same impression on him as on the Cabby and the children. For what you see and hear depends a good deal on where you are standing: it also depends on what sort of person you are.

Ever since the animals had first appeared, Uncle Andrew had been shrinking further and further back into the thicket. He watched them very hard of course; but he wasn't really interested in seeing what they were doing, only in seeing whether they were going to make a rush at him. Like the Witch, he was dreadfully practical. He simply didn't notice that Aslan was choosing one pair out of every kind of beasts. All he saw, or thought he saw, was a lot of dangerous wild animals walking vaguely about. And he kept on wondering why the other animals didn't run away from the big Lion.

When the great moment came and the Beasts spoke, he missed the whole point; for a rather interesting reason. When the Lion had first begun singing, long ago when it was still quite dark, he had realized that the noise was a song. And he had disliked the song very much. It made him think and feel things he did not want to think and feel. Then, when the sun rose and he saw that the singer was a lion ("*only* a lion," as he said to himself) he tried his hardest to make believe that it wasn't singing and never had been singing – only roaring as any lion might in a zoo in our own world. "Of course it can't really have been singing," he thought, "I must have imagined it. I've been letting my nerves get out of order. Who ever heard of a lion singing?" And the longer and more beautiful the Lion sang, the harder Uncle Andrew tried to make himself believe that he could hear nothing but roaring. Now the trouble about trying to make yourself stupider than you really are is that you very often succeed. Uncle Andrew did. He soon did hear nothing but roaring in Aslan's song. Soon he couldn't have heard anything else even if he had wanted to. And when at last the Lion spoke and said, "Narnia awake," he didn't hear any words: he heard only a snarl. And when the Beasts spoke in answer, he heard only barkings, growlings, bayings, and howlings. And when they laughed – well, you can imagine. That was worse for Uncle Andrew than anything that had happened yet. Such a horrid, bloodthirsty din of hungry and angry brutes he had never heard in his life. Then, to his utter rage and horror, he saw the other three humans actually walking out into the open to meet the animals.

"The fools!" he said to himself. "Now those brutes will eat the rings along with the children and I'll never be able to get home again. What a selfish little boy that Digory is! And the others are just as bad. If they want to throw away their own lives, that's their business. But what about *me*? They don't seem to think of that. No one thinks of *me*."

Finally, when a whole crowd of animals came rushing towards him, he turned and ran for his life. And now

anyone could see that the air of that young world was really doing the old gentleman good. In London he had been far too old to run: now, he ran at a speed which would have made him certain to win the hundred yards' race at any Prep school in England. His coat-tails flying out behind him were a fine sight. But of course it was no use. Many of the animals behind him were swift ones; it was the first run they had ever taken in their lives and they were all longing to use their new muscles. "After him! After him!" they shouted. "Perhaps he's that Neevil! Tally-ho! Tantivy! Cut him off! Round him up! Keep it up! Hurrah!"

In a very few minutes some of them got ahead of him. They lined up in a row and barred his way. Others hemmed him in from behind. Wherever he looked he saw terrors. Antlers of great elks and the huge face of an elephant towered over him. Heavy, serious-minded bears and boars grunted behind him. Cool-looking leopards and panthers with sarcastic faces (as he thought) stared at him and waved their tails. What struck him most of all was

the number of open mouths. The animals had really opened their mouths to pant; he thought they had opened their mouths to eat him.

Uncle Andrew stood trembling and swaying this way and that. He had never liked animals at the best of times, being usually rather afraid of them; and of course years of doing cruel experiments on animals had made him hate and fear them far more.

"Now, sir," said the Bulldog in his business-like way, "are you animal, vegetable, or mineral?" That was what it really said; but all Uncle Andrew heard was "Gr-r-r-arrh-ow!"

CHAPTER ELEVEN

DIGORY AND HIS UNCLE ARE BOTH IN TROUBLE

YOU may think the animals were very stupid not to see at once that Uncle Andrew was the same kind of creature as the two children and the Cabby. But you must remember that the animals knew nothing about clothes. They thought that Polly's frock and Digory's Norfolk suit and the Cabby's howlet hat were as much parts of them as their own fur and feathers. They wouldn't have known even that those three were all of the same kind if they hadn't spoken to them and if Strawberry had not seemed to think so. And Uncle Andrew was a great deal taller than the children and a good deal thinner than the Cabby. He was all in black except for his white waistcoat (not very white by now), and the great grey mop of his hair (now very wild indeed) didn't look to them like anything they had seen in the three other humans. So it was only natural that they should be puzzled. Worst of all, he didn't seem to be able to talk.

He had tried to. When the Bulldog spoke to him (or, as he thought, first snarled and then growled at him) he held out his shaking hand and gasped "Good Doggie, then, poor old fellow." But the beasts could not understand him any more than he could understand them. They didn't hear any words: only a vague sizzling noise. Perhaps it was just as well they didn't, for no dog that I ever knew, least of all a Talking Dog of Narnia, likes being called a Good Doggie then; any more than you would like being called My Little Man.

Then Uncle Andrew dropped down in a dead faint.

"There!" said a Warthog, "it's only a tree. I always thought so." (Remember, they had never yet seen a faint or even a fall.)

The Bulldog, who had been sniffing Uncle Andrew all over, raised its head and said, "It's an animal. Certainly an animal. And probably the same kind as those other ones."

"I don't see that," said one of the Bears. "An animal wouldn't just roll over like that. We're animals and *we* don't roll over. We stand up. Like this." He rose to his hind legs, took a step backwards, tripped over a low branch and fell flat on his back.

"The Third Joke, the Third Joke, the Third Joke!" said the Jackdaw in great excitement.

"I still think it's a sort of tree," said the Warthog.

"If it's a tree," said the other Bear, "there might be a bees' nest in it."

"I'm sure it's not a tree," said the Badger. "I had a sort of idea it was trying to speak before it toppled over."

"That was only the wind in its branches," said the Warthog.

"You surely don't mean," said the Jackdaw to the Badger, "that you think its a *talking* animal! It didn't say any words."

"And yet, you know," said the Elephant (the She-Elephant, of course; her husband, as you remember, had been called away by Aslan). "And yet, you know, it might be an animal of some kind. Mightn't the whitish lump at this end be a sort of face? And couldn't those holes be eyes and a mouth? No nose, of course. But then – ahem – one mustn't be narrow-minded. Very few of us have what could exactly be called a Nose." She squinted down the length of her own trunk with pardonable pride.

"I object to that remark very strongly," said the Bulldog.

"The Elephant is quite right," said the Tapir.

"I tell you what!" said the Donkey brightly, "perhaps it's an animal that can't talk but thinks it can."

"Can it be made to stand up?" said the Elephant thoughtfully. She took the limp form of Uncle Andrew gently in her trunk and set him up on end: upside down, unfortunately, so that two half-sovereigns, three half-crowns, and a sixpence fell out of his pocket. But it was no use. Uncle Andrew merely collapsed again.

"There!" said several voices. "It isn't an animal at all. It's not alive."

"I tell you, it *is* an animal," said the Bulldog. "Smell it for yourself."

"Smelling isn't everything," said the Elephant.

"Why," said the Bulldog, "if a fellow can't trust his nose, what is he to trust?"

"Well, his brains perhaps," she replied mildly.

"I object to that remark very strongly," said the Bulldog.

"Well, we must do something about it," said the Elephant. "Because it may be the Neevil, and it must be shown to Aslan. What do most of us think? Is it an animal or something of the tree kind?"

"Tree! Tree!" said a dozen voices.

"Very well," said the Elephant. "Then, if it's a tree it wants to be planted. We must dig a hole."

The two Moles settled that part of the business pretty quickly. There was some dispute as to which way up Uncle Andrew ought to be put into the hole, and he had a very narrow escape from being put in head foremost. Several animals said his legs must be his branches and therefore the grey, fluffy thing (they meant his head) must be his root. But then others said that the forked end of him was the muddier and that it spread out more, as roots ought to do. So finally he was planted right way up. When they had patted down the earth it came up above his knees.

"It looks dreadfully withered," said the Donkey.

"Of course it wants some watering," said the Elephant.

"I think I *might* say (meaning no offence to anyone present) that, perhaps, for *that* sort of work, my kind of nose –"

"I object to that remark very strongly," said the Bulldog. But the Elephant walked quietly to the river, filled her trunk with water, and came back to attend to Uncle Andrew. The sagacious animal went on doing this till gallons of water had been squirted over him, and water was running out of the skirts of his frock-coat as if he had been for a bath with all his clothes on. In the end it revived him. He awoke from his faint. What a wakening it was! But we must leave him to think over his wicked deed (if he was likely to do anything so sensible) and turn to more important things.

Strawberry trotted on with Digory on his back till the noise of the other animals died away, and now the little group of Aslan and his chosen councillors was quite close. Digory knew that he couldn't possibly break in on so solemn a meeting, but there was no need to do so. At a word from Aslan, the He-Elephant, the Ravens, and all the rest of them drew aside. Digory slipped off the horse and found himself face to face with Aslan. And Aslan was bigger and more beautiful amd more brightly golden and more terrible than he had thought. He dared not look into the great eyes.

"Please – Mr Lion – Aslan – Sir," said Digory, "could you – may I – please, will you give me some magic fruit of this country to make Mother well?"

He had been desperately hoping that the Lion would say "Yes"; he had been horribly afraid it might say "No". But he was taken aback when it did neither.

"This is the Boy," said Aslan, looking, not at Digory, but at his councillors. "This is the Boy who did it."

"Oh dear," thought Digory, "what have I done now?"

"Son of Adam," said the Lion. "There is an evil Witch abroad in my new land of Narnia. Tell these good Beasts how she came here."

A dozen different things that he might say flashed through Digory's mind, but he had the sense to say nothing except the exact truth.

"I brought her, Aslan," he answered in a low voice.

"For what purpose?"

"I wanted to get her out of my own world back into her own. I thought I was taking her back to her own place."

"How came she to be in your world, Son of Adam?"

"By – by Magic."

The Lion said nothing and Digory knew that he had not told enough.

"It was my Uncle, Aslan," he said. "He sent us out of our own world by magic rings, at least I had to go because he sent Polly first, and then we met the Witch in a place called Charn and she just held on to us when –"

"You *met* the Witch?" said Aslan in a low voice which had the threat of a growl in it.

"She woke up," said Digory wretchedly. And then, turning very white, "I mean, I woke her. Because I wanted to know what would happen if I struck a bell. Polly didn't want to. It wasn't her fault. I – I fought her. I know I shouldn't have. I think I was a bit enchanted by the writing under the bell."

"Do you?" asked Aslan; still speaking very low and deep.

"No," said Digory. "I see now I wasn't. I was only pretending."

There was a long pause. And Digory was thinking all the time, "I've spoiled everything. There's no chance of getting anything for Mother now."

When the Lion spoke again, it was not to Digory.

"You see, friends," he said, "that before the new, clean world I gave you is seven hours old, a force of evil has already entered it; waked and brought hither by this son of Adam." The Beasts, even Strawberry, all turned their eyes on Digory till he felt that he wished the ground would swallow him up. "But do not be cast down," said Aslan, still speaking to the Beasts. "Evil will come of that evil, but it is still a long way off, and I will see to it that the worst falls upon myself. In the meantime, let us take such order that for many hundred years yet this shall be a merry land in a merry world. And as Adam's race has done the harm, Adam's race shall help to heal it. Draw near, you other two."

The last words were spoken to Polly and the Cabby who had now arrived. Polly, all eyes and mouth, was staring at Aslan and holding the Cabby's hand rather tightly. The Cabby gave one glance at the Lion, and took off his bowler hat: no one had yet seen him without it. When it was off, he looked younger and nicer, and more like a countryman and less like a London cabman.

"Son," said Aslan to the Cabby. "I have known you long. Do you know me?"

"Well, no, sir," said the Cabby. "Leastways, not in an ordinary manner of speaking. Yet I feel somehow, if I may make so free, as 'ow we've met before."

"It is well," said the Lion. "You know better than you think you know, and you shall live to know me better yet. How does this land please you?"

"It's a fair treat, sir," said the Cabby.

"Would you like to live here always?"

"Well you see sir, I'm a married man," said the Cabby. "If my wife was here neither of us would ever want to go back to London, I reckon. We're both country folks really."

Aslan threw up his shaggy head, opened his mouth, and uttered a long, single note; not very loud, but full of power. Polly's heart jumped in her body when she heard it. She felt sure that it was a call, and that anyone who heard that call would want to obey it and (what's more) would be able to obey it, however many worlds and ages lay between. And so, though she was filled with wonder, she was not really astonished or shocked when all of a sudden a young woman, with a kind, honest face stepped out of nowhere and stood beside her. Polly knew at once that it was the Cabby's wife, fetched out of our world not by any tiresome magic rings, but quickly, simply and sweetly as a bird flies to its nest. The young woman had apparently been in the middle of a washing day, for she wore an apron, her sleeves were rolled up to the elbow, and there were soapsuds on her hands. If she had had time to put on her good clothes (her best hat had imitation cherries on it) she would have looked dreadful; as it was, she looked rather nice.

Of course she thought she was dreaming. That was why she didn't rush across to her husband and ask him what on earth had happened to them both. But when she looked at the Lion she didn't feel quite so sure it was a

dream, yet for some reason she did not appear to be very frightened. Then she dropped a little half curtsey, as some country girls still knew how to do in those days. After that, she went and put her hand in the Cabby's and stood there looking round her a little shyly.

"My children," said Aslan, fixing his eyes on both of them, "you are to be the first King and Queen of Narnia."

The Cabby opened his mouth in astonishment, and his wife turned very red.

"You shall rule and name all these creatures, and do justice among them, and protect them from their enemies when enemies arise. And enemies will arise, for there is an evil Witch in this world."

The Cabby swallowed hard two or three times and cleared his throat.

"Begging your pardon, sir," he said, "and thanking you very much I'm sure (which my Missus does the same) but I ain't no sort of a chap for a job like that. I never 'ad much eddycation, you see."

"Well," said Aslan,"can you use a spade and a plough and raise food out of the earth?"

"Yes, sir, I could do a bit of that sort of work: being brought up to it, like."

"Can you rule these creatures kindly and fairly, remembering that they are not slaves like the dumb beasts of the world you were born in, but Talking Beasts and free subjects?"

"I see that, sir," replied the Cabby. "I'd try to do the square thing by them all."

"And would you bring up your children and grandchildren to do the same?"

"It'd be up to me to try, sir. I'd do my best: wouldn't we, Nellie?"

"And you wouldn't have favourites either among your own children or among the other creatures or let any hold another under or use it hardly?"

"I never could abide such goings on, sir, and that's the truth. I'd give 'em what for if I caught 'em at it," said the Cabby. (All through this conversation his voice was growing slower and richer. More like the country voice he must have had as a boy and less like the sharp, quick voice of a cockney.)

"And if enemies came against the land (for enemies will arise) and there was war, would you be the first in the charge and the last in the retreat?"

"Well, sir," said the Cabby very slowly, "a chap don't exactly know till he's been tried. I dare say I might turn out ever such a soft 'un. Never did no fighting except with my fists. I'd try – that is, I 'ope I'd try – to do my bit."

"Then," said Aslan, "You will have done all that a King should do. Your coronation will be held presently. And you and your children and grandchildren shall be blessed, and some will be Kings of Narnia, and others will be Kings of Archenland which lies yonder over the Southern Mountains. And you, little Daughter (here he turned to Polly) are welcome. Have you forgiven the Boy for the violence he did you in the Hall of Images in the desolate palace of accursed Charn?"

"Yes, Aslan, we've made it up," said Polly.

"That is well," said Aslan. "And now for the Boy himself."

CHAPTER TWELVE

STRAWBERRY'S ADVENTURE

DIGORY kept his mouth very tight shut. He had been growing more and more uncomfortable. He hoped that, whatever happened, he wouldn't blub or do anything ridiculous.

"Son of Adam," said Aslan. "Are you ready to undo the wrong that you have done to my sweet country of Narnia on the very day of its birth?"

"Well, I don't see what I can do," said Digory. "You see, the Queen ran away and –"

"I asked, are you ready?" said the Lion.

"Yes," said Digory. He had had for a second some wild idea of saying "I'll try to help you if you'll promise to help my Mother," but he realized in time that the Lion was not at all the sort of person one could try to make bargains with. But when he had said "Yes," he thought of his Mother, and he thought of the great hopes he had had, and how they were all dying away, and a lump came in his throat and tears in his eyes, and he blurted out:

"But please, please – won't you – can't you give me something that will cure Mother?" Up till then he had been looking at the Lion's great feet and the huge claws on them; now, in his despair, he looked up at its face. What he saw surprised him as much as anything in his whole life. For the tawny face was bent down near his own and (wonder of wonders) great shining tears stood in the Lion's eyes. They were such big, bright tears compared with Digory's own that for a moment he felt as if the Lion must really be sorrier about his Mother than he was himself.

"My son, my son," said Aslan. "I know. Grief is great. Only you and I in this land know that yet. Let us be good to one another. But I have to think of hundreds of years in the life of Narnia. The Witch whom you have brought into this world will come back to Narnia again. But it need not be yet. It is my wish to plant in Narnia a tree that she will not dare to approach, and that tree will protect Narnia from her for many years. So this land shall have a long, bright morning before any clouds come over the sun. You must get me the seed from which that tree is to grow."

"Yes, sir," said Digory. He didn't know how it was to be done but he felt quite sure now that he would be able to do it. The Lion drew a deep breath, stooped its head even lower and gave him a Lion's kiss. And at once Digory felt that new strength and courage had gone into him.

"Dear son," said Aslan, "I will tell you what you must do. Turn and look to the West and tell me what do you see?"

"I see terribly big mountains, Aslan," said Digory, "I see this river coming down cliffs in a waterfall. And beyond the cliff there are high green hills with forests. And beyond those there are higher ranges that look almost black. And then, far away, there are big snowy mountains all heaped up together – like pictures of the Alps. And behind those there's nothing but the sky."

"You see well," said the Lion. "Now the land of Narnia ends where the waterfall comes down, and once you have reached the top of the cliffs you will be out of Narnia and into the Western Wild. You must journey through those mountains till you find a green valley with a blue lake in it, walled round by mountains of ice. At the end of the lake there is a steep, green hill. On the top of that hill there is a garden. In the centre of that garden is a tree. Pluck an apple from that tree and bring it back to me."

"Yes, sir," said Digory again. He hadn't the least idea of how he was to climb the cliff and find his way among all the mountains, but he didn't like to say that for fear it would sound like making excuses. But he did say, "I hope, Aslan, you're not in a hurry. I shan't be able to get there and back very quickly."

"Little son of Adam, you shall have help," said Aslan. He then turned to the Horse who had been standing quietly beside them all this time, swishing his tail to keep the flies off, and listening with his head on one side as if the conversation were a little difficult to understand.

"My dear," said Aslan to the Horse, "would you like to be a winged horse?"

You should have seen how the Horse shook its mane and how its nostrils widened, and the little tap it gave the ground with one back hoof. Clearly it would very much like to be a winged horse. But it only said:

"If you wish, Aslan – if you really mean – I don't know why it should be me – I'm not a very clever horse."

"Be winged. Be the father of all flying horses," roared Aslan in a voice that shook the ground. "Your name is Fledge."

The horse shied, just as it might have shied in the old, miserable days when it pulled a hansom. Then it roared. It strained its neck back as if there were a fly biting its shoulders and it wanted to scratch them. And then, just as the beasts had burst out of the earth, there burst out from the shoulders of Fledge wings that spread and grew, larger than eagles', larger than swans', larger than angels' wings

in church windows. The feathers shone chestnut colour and copper colour. He gave a great sweep with them and leaped into the air. Twenty feet above Aslan and Digory he snorted, neighed, and curvetted. Then, after circling once round them, he dropped to the earth, all four hoofs together, looking awkward and surprised, but extremely pleased.

"Is it good, Fledge?" said Aslan.

"It is very good, Aslan," said Fledge.

"Will you carry this little son of Adam on your back to the mountain-valley I spoke of?"

"What? Now? At once?" said Strawberry – or Fledge, as we must now call him – "Hurrah! Come on little one, I've had things like you on my back before.

Long, long ago. When there were green fields; and sugar."

"What are the two daughters of Eve whispering about?" said Aslan, turning very suddenly on Polly and the Cabby's wife, who had in fact been making friends.

"If you please, sir," said Queen Helen (for that is what Nellie the cabman's wife now was), "I think the little girl would love to go too, if it weren't no trouble."

"What does Fledge say about that?" asked the Lion.

"Oh, I don't mind two, not when they're little ones," said Fledge. "But I hope the Elephant doesn't want to come as well."

The Elephant had no such wish, and the new King of Narnia helped both the children up: that is, he gave Digory a rough heave and set Polly as gently and daintily on the horse's back as if she were made of china and might break. "There they are, Strawberry – Fledge, I should say. This is a rum go."

"Do not fly too high," said Aslan. "Do not try to go over the tops of the great ice-mountains. Look out for the valleys, the green places, and fly through them. There will always be a way through. And now, begone with my blessing."

"Oh Fledge!" said Digory, leaning forward to pat the Horse's glossy neck. "This *is* fun. Hold on to me tight, Polly."

Next moment the country dropped away beneath them, and whirled round as Fledge, like a huge pigeon, circled once or twice before setting off on his long westward flight. Looking down, Polly could hardly see the King and the Queen, and even Aslan himself was only a bright yellow spot on the green grass. Soon the wind was in their faces and Fledge's wings settled down to a steady beat.

All Narnia, many-coloured with lawns and rocks and heather and different sorts of trees, lay spread out below them, the river winding through it like a ribbon of quicksilver. They could already see over the tops of the low hills which lay northward on their right; beyond those hills a great moorland sloped gently up and up to the horizon. On their left the mountains were much higher, but every now and then there was a gap when you could see, between steep pine woods, a glimpse of the southern lands that lay beyond them, looking blue and far away.

"That'll be where Archenland is," said Polly.

"Yes, but look ahead!" said Digory.

For now a great barrier of cliffs rose before them and they were almost dazzled by the sunlight dancing on the great waterfall by which the river roars and sparkles down into Narnia itself from the high western lands in which it rises. They were flying so high already that the thunder of those falls could only just be heard as a small, thin sound, but they were not yet high enough to fly over the top of the cliffs.

"We'll have to do a bit of zig-zagging here," said Fledge. "Hold on tight."

He began flying to and fro, getting higher at each turn. The air grew colder, and they heard the call of eagles far below them.

"I say, look back! Look behind," said Polly.

There they could see the whole valley of Narnia stretched out to where, just before the eastern horizon, there was a gleam of the sea. And now they were so high that they could see tiny-looking jagged mountains appearing beyond the northwest moors, and plains of what looked like sand far in the south.

"I wish we had someone to tell us what all those places are," said Digory.

"I don't suppose they're anywhere yet," said Polly. "I mean, there's no one there, and nothing happening. The world only began today."

"No, but people *will* get there," said Digory. "And then they'll have histories, you know."

"Well, it's a jolly good thing they haven't now," said Polly. "Because nobody can be made to learn it. Battles and dates and all that rot."

Now they were over the top of the cliffs and in a few minutes the valley land of Narnia had sunk out of sight behind them. They were flying over a wild country of steep hills and dark forests, still following the course of the river. The really big mountains loomed ahead. But the sun was now in the travellers' eyes and they couldn't see things very clearly in that direction. For the sun sank lower and lower till the western sky was all like one great furnace full of melted gold; and it set at last behind a jagged peak which stood up against the brightness as sharp and flat as if it were cut out of cardboard.

"It's none too warm up here," said Polly.

"And my wings are beginning to ache," said Fledge. There's no sign of the valley with a Lake in it, like what Aslan said. What about coming down and looking out for a decent spot to spend the night in? We shan't reach that place tonight."

"Yes, and surely it's about time for supper?" said Digory.

So Fledge came lower and lower. As they came down nearer to the earth and among the hills, the air grew warmer and after travelling so many hours with nothing to listen to but the beat of Fledge's wings, it was nice to hear the homely and earthy noises again – the chatter of the river on its stony bed and the creaking of trees in the light wind. A warm, good smell of sun-baked earth and grass and flowers came up to them. At last Fledge alighted. Digory rolled off and helped Polly to dismount. Both were glad to stretch their stiff legs.

The valley in which they had come down was in the heart of the mountains; snowy heights, one of them looking rose-red in the reflections of the sunset, towered above them.

"I *am* hungry," said Digory.

"Well, tuck in," said Fledge, taking a big mouthful of grass. Then he raised his head, still chewing and with bits of grass sticking out on each side of his mouth like whiskers, and said, "Come on, you two. Don't be shy. There's plenty for us all."

"But we can't eat grass," said Digory.

"H'm, h'm," said Fledge, speaking with his mouth full. "Well – h'm – don't know quite what you'll do then. Very good grass too."

Polly and Digory stared at one another in dismay.

"Well, I *do* think someone might have arranged about our meals," said Digory.

"I'm sure Aslan would have, if you'd asked him," said Fledge.

"Wouldn't he know without being asked?" said Polly.

"I've no doubt he would," said the Horse (still with his mouth full). "But I've a sort of idea he likes to be asked."

"But what on earth are we to do?" asked Digory.

"I'm sure I don't know," said Fledge. "Unless you try the grass. You might like it better than you think."

"Oh, don't be silly," said Polly, stamping her foot. "Of

course humans can't eat grass, any more than you could eat a mutton chop."

"For goodness' sake don't talk about chops and things," said Digory. "It only makes it worse."

Digory said that Polly had better take herself home by ring and get something to eat there; he couldn't himself because he had promised to go straight on his message for Aslan, and, if once he showed up again at home, anything might happen to prevent his getting back. But Polly said she wouldn't leave him, and Digory said it was jolly decent of her.

"I say," said Polly, "I've still got the remains of that bag of toffee in my jacket. It'll be better than nothing."

"A lot better," said Digory, "But be careful to get your hand into your pocket without touching your ring."

This was a difficult and delicate job but they managed it in the end. The little paper bag was very squashy and sticky when they finally got it out, so that it was more a question of tearing the bag off the toffees than of getting the toffees out of the bag. Some grown-ups (you know how fussy they can be about that sort of thing) would rather have gone without supper altogether than eaten those toffees. There were nine of them all told. It was Digory who had the bright idea of eating four each and planting the ninth; for, as he said, "if the bar off the lamp-post turned into a little light-tree, why shouldn't this turn into a toffee-tree?" So they dibbled a small hole in the turf and buried the piece of toffee. Then they ate the other pieces, making them last as long as they could. It was a poor meal, even with all the paper they couldn't help eating as well.

When Fledge had quite finished his own excellent supper he lay down. The children came and sat one on each side of him leaning against his warm body, and when he had spread a wing over each they were really quite snug. As the bright young stars of that new world came out they talked over everything: how Digory had hoped to get something for his Mother and how, instead of that, he had been sent on this message. And they repeated to one another all the signs by which they would

know the places they were looking for – the blue lake and the hill with a garden on top of it. The talk was just beginning to slow down as they got sleepy, when suddenly Polly sat up wide awake and said "Hush!"

Everyone listened as hard as they could.

"Perhaps it was only the wind in the trees," said Digory presently.

"I'm not so sure," said Fledge. "Anyway – wait! There it goes again. By Aslan, it *is* something."

The horse scrambled to its feet with a great noise and a great unheaval; the children were already on theirs. Fledge trotted to and fro, sniffing and whinnying. The children tip-toed this way and that, looking behind every bush and tree. They kept on thinking they saw things, and there was one time when Polly was perfectly certain she had seen a tall, dark figure gliding quickly away in a westerly direction. But they caught nothing and in the end Fledge lay down again and the children re-snuggled (if that is the right word) under his wings. They went to sleep at once. Fledge stayed awake much longer moving his ears to and fro in the darkness and sometimes giving a little shiver with his skin as if a fly had lighted on him: but in the end he too slept.

CHAPTER THIRTEEN

AN UNEXPECTED MEETING

"Wake up, Digory, wake up, Fledge," came the voice of Polly. "It *has* turned into a toffee tree. And it's the loveliest morning."

The low early sunshine was streaming through the wood and the grass was grey with dew and the cobwebs were like silver. Just beside them was a little, very dark-wooded tree, about the size of an apple tree. The leaves were whitish and rather papery, like the herb called honesty, and it was loaded with little brown fruits that looked rather like dates.

"Hurrah!" said Digory. "But I'm going to have a dip first." He rushed through a flowering thicket or two down to the river's edge. Have you ever bathed in a mountain river that is running in shallow cataracts over red and blue and yellow stones with the sun on it? It is as good as the sea: in some ways almost better. Of course, he had to dress again without drying but it was well worth it. When he came back, Polly went down and had her bathe; at least she said that was what she'd been doing, but we know she was not much of a swimmer and perhaps it is best not to ask too many questions. Fledge visited the river too but he only stood in midstream, stooping down for a long drink of water and then shaking his mane and neighing several times.

Polly and Digory got to work on the toffee-tree. The fruit was delicious; not exactly like toffee – softer for one thing, and juicy – but like fruit which reminded one of toffee. Fledge also made an excellent breakfast; he tried one of the toffee fruits and liked it but said he felt more like grass at that hour in the morning. Then with some difficulty the children got on his back and the second journey began.

It was even better than yesterday, partly because every one was feeling so fresh, and partly because the newly risen sun was at their backs and, of course, everything looks nicer when the light is behind you. It was a wonderful ride. The big snowy mountains rose above them in every direction. The valleys, far beneath them, were so green, and all the streams which tumbled down from the glaciers into the main river were so blue, that it was like flying over gigantic pieces of jewellery. They would have liked this part of the adventure to go on longer than it did. But quite soon they were all sniffing the air and saying "What is it?" and "Did you smell something?" and "Where's it coming from?" For a heavenly smell, warm and golden, as if from all the most delicious fruits and flowers of the world, was coming up to them from somewhere ahead.

"It's coming from that valley with the lake in it," said Fledge.

"So it is," said Digory. "And look! There's a green hill at the far end of the lake. And look how blue the water is."

"It must be the Place," said all three.

Fledge came lower and lower in wide circles. The icy peaks rose up higher and higher above. The air came up warmer and sweeter every moment, so sweet that it almost brought the tears to your eyes. Fledge was now gliding with his wings spread out motionless on each side, and his hoofs pawing for the ground. The steep green hill was rushing towards them. A moment later he alighted on its slope, a little awkwardly. The children rolled off, fell

without hurting themselves on the warm, fine grass, and stood up panting a little.

They were three-quarters of the way up the hill, and set out at once to climb to the top. (I don't think Fledge could have managed this without his wings to balance him and to give him the help of a flutter now and then.) All round the very top of the hill ran a high wall of green turf. Inside the wall trees were growing. Their branches hung out over the wall; their leaves showed not only green but also blue and silver when the wind stirred them. When the travellers reached the top they walked nearly all the way round it outside the green wall before they found the gates: high gates of gold, fast shut, facing due east.

Up till now I think Fledge and Polly had had the idea that they would go in with Digory. But they thought so no longer. You never saw a place which was so obviously private. You could see at a glance that it belonged to someone else. Only a fool would dream of going in unless he had been sent there on very special business. Digory himself understood at once that the others wouldn't and couldn't come in with him. He went forward to the gates alone.

When he had come close up to them he saw words written on the gold with silver letters; something like this:

Come in by the gold gates or not at all,
Take of my fruit for others or forbear,
For those who steal or those who climb my wall
Shall find their heart's desire and find despair.

"*Take of my fruit for others*," said Digory to himself. "Well, that's what I'm going to do. It means I mustn't eat any myself, I suppose. I don't know what all that jaw in the last line is about. *Come in by the gold gates*. Well who'd want to climb a wall if he could get in by a gate! But how do the gates open?" He laid his hand on them and instantly they swung apart, opening inwards, turning on their hinges without the least noise.

Now that he could see into the place it looked more private than ever. He went in very solemnly, looking about him. Everything was very quiet inside. Even the fountain which rose near the middle of the garden made only the faintest sound. The lovely smell was all round him: it was a happy place but very serious.

He knew which was the right tree at once, partly because it stood in the very centre and partly because the great silver apples with which it was loaded shone so and cast a light of their own down on the shadowy places where the sunlight did not reach. He walked straight across to it, picked an apple, and put it in the breast pocket of his Norfolk jacket. But he couldn't help looking at it and smelling it before he put it away.

It would have been better if he had not. A terrible thirst and hunger came over him and a longing to taste that fruit. He put it hastily into his pocket; but there were plenty of others. Could it be wrong to taste one? After all, he thought, the notice on the gate might not have been exactly an order; it might have been only a piece of advice – and who cares about advice? Or even if it were an order, would he be disobeying it by eating an apple? He had already obeyed the part about taking one "for others".

While he was thinking of all this he happened to look up through the branches towards the top of the tree. There, on a branch above his head, a wonderful bird was roosting. I say "roosting" because it seemed almost asleep; perhaps not quite. The tiniest slit of one eye was open. It was larger than an eagle, its breast saffron, its head crested with scarlet, and its tail purple.

"And it just shows," said Digory afterwards when he was telling the story to the others, "that you can't be too careful in these magical places. You never know what may be watching you." But I think Digory would not have taken an apple for himself in any case. Things like Do Not Steal were, I think, hammered into boys' heads a good deal harder in those days than they are now. Still, we can never be certain.

Digory was just turning to go back to the gates when he stopped to have one last look around. He got a terrible shock. He was not alone. There, only a few yards away from him, stood the Witch. She was just throwing away the core of an apple which she had eaten. The juice was darker than you would expect and had made a horrid stain round her mouth. Digory guessed at once that she must have climbed in over the wall. And he began to see that there might be some sense in that last line about getting your heart's desire and getting despair along with it. For the Witch looked stronger and prouder than ever, and even, in a way, triumphant; but her face was deadly white, white as salt.

All this flashed through Digory's mind in a second; then he took to his heels and ran for the gates as hard as he could pelt; the Witch after him. As soon as he was out, the gates closed behind him of their own accord. That gave him the lead but not for long. By the time he had reached the others and was shouting out "Quick, get on, Polly! Get up, Fledge", the Witch had climbed the wall, or vaulted over it, and was close behind him again.

"Stay where you are," cried Digory, turning round to face her, "or we'll all vanish. Don't come an inch nearer."

"Foolish boy," said the Witch. "Why do you run from me? I mean you no harm. If you do not stop and listen to me now, you will miss some knowledge that would have made you happy all your life."

"Well I don't want to hear it, thanks," said Digory. But he did.

"I know what errand you have come on," continued the Witch. "For it was I who was close beside you in the woods last night and heard all your counsels. You have plucked fruit in the garden yonder. You have it in your pocket now. And you are going to carry it back, untasted, to the Lion; for *him* to eat, for *him* to use. You simpleton! Do you know what that fruit is? I will tell you. It is the apple of youth, the apple of life. I know, for I have tasted it; and I feel already such changes in myself that I know I shall never grow old or die. Eat it, Boy, eat it; and you and I will both live forever and be king and queen of this whole world – or of your world, if we decide to go back there."

"No thanks," said Digory, "I don't know that I care much about living on and on after everyone I know is dead. I'd rather live an ordinary time and die and go to Heaven."

"But what about this Mother of yours whom you pretend to love so?"

"What's she got to do with it?" said Digory.

"Do you not see, Fool, that one bite of that apple would heal her? You have it in your pocket. We are here by ourselves and the Lion is far away. Use your Magic and go back to your own world. A minute later you can be at your Mother's bedside, giving her the fruit. Five minutes later you will see the colour coming back to her face. She will tell you the pain is gone. Soon she will tell you she feels stronger. Then she will fall asleep – think of that; hours of sweet natural sleep, without pain, without drugs. Next day everyone will be saying how wonderfully she has recovered. Soon she will be quite well again. All will be well again. Your home will be happy again. You will be like other boys."

"Oh!" gasped Digory as if he had been hurt, and put his hand to his head. For he now knew that the most terrible choice lay before him.

"What has the Lion ever done for you that you should

be his slave?" said the Witch. "What can he do to you once you are back in your own world? And what would your Mother think if she knew that you *could* have taken her pain away and given her back her life and saved your Father's heart from being broken, and that you *wouldn't* – that you'd rather run messages for a wild animal in a strange world that is no business of yours?"

"I – I don't think he is a wild animal," said Digory in a dried-up sort of voice. "He is – I don't know –"

"Then he is something worse," said the Witch. "Look what he has done to you already; look how heartless he has made you. That is what he does to everyone who listens to him. Cruel, pitiless boy! you would let your own Mother die rather than –"

"Oh shut up," said the miserable Digory, still in the same voice. "Do you think I don't see? But I – I promised."

"Ah, but you didn't know what you were promising. And no one here can prevent you."

"Mother herself," said Digory, getting the words out with difficulty, "wouldn't like it – awfully strict about keeping promises – and not stealing – and all that sort of thing. *She'd* tell me not to do it – quick as anything – if she was here."

"But she need never know," said the Witch, speaking more sweetly than you would have thought anyone with so fierce a face could speak. "You wouldn't tell her how you'd got the apple. Your Father need never know. No one in your world need know anything about this whole story. You needn't take the little girl back with you, you know."

That was where the Witch made her fatal mistake. Of course Digory knew that Polly could get away by her own ring as easily as he could get away by his. But apparently the Witch didn't know this. And the meanness of the suggestion that he should leave Polly behind suddenly made all the other things the Witch had been saying to him sound false and hollow. And even in the midst of all his misery, his head suddenly cleared, and he said (in a different and much louder voice):

"Look here; where do *you* come into all this? Why are *you* so precious fond of *my* Mother all of a sudden? What's it got to do with you? What's your game?"

"Good for you, Digs," whispered Polly in his ear. "Quick! Get away *now*." She hadn't dared to say anything all through the argument because, you see, it wasn't *her* Mother who was dying.

"Up then," said Digory, heaving her on to Fledge's back and then scrambling up as quickly as he could. The horse spread its wings.

"Go then, Fools," called the Witch. "Think of me, Boy, when you lie old and weak and dying, and remember how you threw away the chance of endless youth! It won't be offered you again."

They were already so high that they could only just hear her. Nor did the Witch waste any time gazing up at them; they saw her set off northward down the slope of the hill.

They had started early that morning and what happened in the garden had not taken very long, so that Fledge and Polly both said they would easily get back to Narnia before nightfall. Digory never spoke on the way back, and the others were shy of speaking to him. He was very sad and he wasn't even sure all the time that he had done the right thing; but whenever he remembered the shining tears in Aslan's eyes he became sure.

All day Fledge flew steadily with untiring wings; eastward with the river to guide him, through the mountains and over the wild wooded hills, and then over the great waterfall and down, and down, to where the woods of Narnia were darkened by the shadow of the mighty cliff, till at last, when the sky was growing red with sunset behind them, he saw a place where many creatures were gathered together by the riverside. And soon he could see Aslan himself in the midst of them. Fledge glided down, spread out his four legs, closed his wings, and landed cantering. Then he pulled up. The children dismounted. Digory saw all the animals, dwarfs, satyrs, nymphs, and other things drawing back to the left and right to make way for him. He walked up to Aslan, handed him the apple and said:

"I've brought you the apple you wanted, sir."

CHAPTER FOURTEEN

THE PLANTING OF THE TREE

"WELL done," said Aslan in a voice that made the earth shake. Then Digory knew that all the Narnians had heard those words and that the story of them would be handed down from father to son in that new world for hundreds of years and perhaps forever. But he was in no danger of feeling conceited for he didn't think about it at all now that he was face to face with Aslan. This time he found he could look straight into the Lion's eyes. He had forgotten his troubles and felt absolutely content.

"Well done, son of Adam," said the Lion again. "For this fruit you have hungered and thirsted and wept. No hand but yours shall sow the seed of the Tree that is to be the protection of Narnia. Throw the apple towards the river bank where the ground is soft."

Digory did as he was told. Everyone had grown so quiet that you could hear the soft thump where it fell into the mud.

"It is well thrown," said Aslan. "Let us now proceed to the Coronation of King Frank of Narnia and Helen his Queen."

The children now noticed these two for the first time. They were dressed in strange and beautiful clothes, and from their shoulders rich robes flowed out behind them to where four dwarfs held up the King's train and four river-nymphs the Queen's. Their heads were bare; but Helen had let her hair down and it made a great improvement in her appearance. But it was neither hair nor clothes that made them look so different from their old selves. Their faces had a new expression, especially the King's. All the sharpness and cunning and quarrelsomeness which he had picked up as a London cabby seemed to have been washed away, and the courage and kindness which he had always had were easier to see. Perhaps it was the air of the young world that had done it, or talking with Aslan, or both.

"Upon my word," whispered Fledge to Polly. "My old master's been changed nearly as much as I have! Why, he's a real master now."

"Yes, but don't buzz in my ear like that," said Polly. "It tickles so."

"Now," said Aslan, "some of you undo that tangle you have made with those trees and let us see what we shall find there."

Digory now saw that where four trees grew close together their branches had all been laced together or tied together with switches so as to make a sort of cage. The two Elephants with their trunks and a few dwarfs with their little axes soon got it all undone. There were three things inside. One was a young tree that seemed to be made of gold; the second was a young tree that seemed to be made of silver; but the third was a miserable object in muddy clothes, sitting hunched up between them.

"Gosh!" whispered Digory. "Uncle Andrew!"

To explain all this we must go back a bit. The Beasts, you remember, had tried planting and watering him. When the watering brought him to his senses, he found himself soaking wet, buried up to his thighs in earth (which was quickly turning into mud) and surrounded by more wild animals than he had ever dreamed of in his life before. It is perhaps not surprising that he began to scream and howl. This was in a way a good thing, for it at last persuaded everyone (even the Warthog) that he was alive. So they dug him up again (his trousers were in a really shocking state by now). As soon as his legs were free he tried to bolt, but one swift curl of the Elephant's trunk round his waist soon put an end to that. Everyone now thought he must be safely kept somewhere till Aslan had time to come and see him and say what should be

done about him. So they made a sort of cage or coop all round him. They then offered him everything they could think of to eat.

The Donkey collected great piles of thistles and threw them in, but Uncle Andrew didn't seem to care about them. The Squirrels bombarded him with volleys of nuts, but he only covered his head with his hands and tried to keep out of the way. Several birds flew to and fro diligently dropping worms on him. The Bear was especially kind. During the afternoon he found a wild bees' nest and instead of eating it himself (which he would very much like to have done) this worthy creature brought it back to Uncle Andrew. But this was in fact the worst failure of all. The Bear lobbed the whole sticky mass over the top of the enclosure and unfortunately it hit Uncle Andrew slap in the face (not all the bees were dead). The Bear, who would not at all have minded being hit in the face by a honeycomb himself, could not understand why Uncle Andrew staggered back, slipped, and sat down. And it was sheer bad luck that he sat down on the pile of thistles. "And anyway," as the Warthog said, "quite a lot of honey has got into the creature's mouth and that's bound to have done it some good." They were really getting quite fond of their strange pet and hoped that Aslan would allow them to keep it. The cleverer ones were quite sure by now that at least some of the noises which came out of his mouth had a meaning. They christened him Brandy because he made that noise so often.

In the end, however, they had to leave him there for the night. Aslan was busy all that day instructing the new King and Queen and doing other important things, and could not attend to "poor old Brandy". What with the nuts, pears, apples, and bananas that had been thrown in to him, he did fairly well for supper; but it wouldn't be true to say that he passed an agreeable night.

"Bring out that creature," said Aslan. One of the Elephants lifted Uncle Andrew in its trunk and laid him at the Lion's feet. He was too frightened to move.

"Please, Aslan," said Polly, "could you say something to – to unfrighten him? And then could you say something to prevent him from ever coming back here again?"

"Do you think he *wants* to?" said Aslan.

"Well, Aslan," said Polly, "he might send someone else. He's so excited about the bar off the lamp-post growing into a lamp-post tree and he thinks –"

"He thinks great folly, child," said Aslan. "This world is bursting with life for these few days because the song with which I called it into life still hangs in the air and rumbles in the ground. It will not be so for long. But I cannot tell that to this old sinner, and I cannot comfort him either; he has made himself unable to hear my voice. If I spoke to him, he would hear only growlings and roarings. Oh Adam's sons, how cleverly you defend yourselves against all that might do you good! But I will give him the only gift he is still able to receive."

He bowed his great head rather sadly, and breathed into the Magician's terrified face. "Sleep," he said. "Sleep and be separated for some few hours from all the torments you have devised for yourself." Uncle Andrew immediately rolled over with closed eyes and began breathing peacefully.

"Carry him aside and lay him down," said Aslan. "Now, dwarfs! Show your smith-craft. Let me see you make two crowns for your King and Queen."

More Dwarfs than you could dream of rushed forward to the Golden Tree. They had all its leaves stripped off, and some of its branches torn off too, before you could say Jack Robinson. And now the children could see that it did not merely look golden but was of real, soft gold. It had of course sprung up from the half-sovereigns which had fallen out of Uncle Andrew's pocket when he was turned upside down; just as the silver had grown up from the half-crowns. From nowhere, as it seemed, piles of dry brushwood for fuel, a little anvil, hammers, tongs, and bellows were produced. Next moment (how those dwarfs loved their work!) the fire was blazing, the bellows were roaring, the gold was melting, the hammers were clinking. Two Moles, whom Aslan had set to dig (which was what they liked best) earlier in the day, poured out a pile of

precious stones at the dwarfs' feet. Under the clever fingers of the little smiths two crowns took shape – not ugly, heavy things like modern European crowns, but light, delicate, beautifully shaped circles that you could really wear and look nicer by wearing. The King's was set with rubies and the Queen's with emeralds.

When the crowns had been cooled in the river Aslan made Frank and Helen kneel before him and he placed the crowns on their heads. Then he said, "Rise up King and Queen of Narnia, father and mother of many kings that shall be in Narnia and the Isles and Archenland. Be just and merciful and brave. The blessing is upon you."

Then everyone cheered or bayed or neighed or

trumpeted or clapped its wings and the royal pair stood looking solemn and a little shy, but all the nobler for their shyness. And while Digory was still cheering he heard the deep voice of Aslan beside him, saying:

"Look!"

Everyone in that crowd turned its head, and then everyone drew a long breath of wonder and delight. A little way off, towering over their heads, they saw a tree which had certainly not been there before. It must have grown up silently, yet swiftly as a flag rises when you pull it up on a flagstaff, while they were all busied about the coronation. Its spreading branches seemed to cast a light rather than a shade, and silver apples peeped out like stars from under every leaf. But it was the smell which came from it, even more than the sight, that had made everyone draw in their breath. For a moment one could hardly think about anything else.

"Son of Adam," said Aslan, "you have sown well. And you, Narnians, let it be your first care to guard this Tree, for it is your Shield. The Witch of whom I told you has fled far away into the North of the world; she will live on there, growing stronger in dark Magic. But while that Tree flourishes she will never come down into Narnia. She dare not come within a hundred miles of the Tree, for its smell, which is joy and life and health to you, is death and horror and despair to her."

Everyone was staring solemnly at the Tree when Aslan suddenly swung round his head (scattering golden gleams of light from his mane as he did so) and fixed his large eyes on the children. "What is it, children?" he said, for he caught them in the very act of whispering and nudging one another.

"Oh – Aslan, sir," said Digory, turning red, "I forgot to

tell you. The Witch has already eaten one of those apples, one of the same kind that Tree grew from." He hadn't really said all he was thinking, but Polly at once said it for him (Digory was always much more afraid than she of looking a fool.)

"So we thought, Aslan," she said, "that there must be some mistake, and she can't really mind the smell of those apples."

"Why do you think that, Daughter of Eve?" asked the Lion.

"Well, she ate one."

"Child," he replied, "that is why all the rest are now a horror to her. That is what happens to those who pluck and eat fruits at the wrong time and in the wrong way. The fruit is good, but they loathe it ever after."

"Oh I see," said Polly. "And I suppose because she took it in the wrong way it won't work for her. I mean it won't make her always young and all that?"

"Alas," said Aslan, shaking his head. "It will. Things always work according to their nature. She has won her heart's desire; she has unwearying strength and endless days like a goddess. But length of days with an evil heart is only length of misery and already she begins to know it. All get what they want; they do not always like it."

"I – I nearly ate one myself, Aslan," said Digory. "Would I –"

"You would, child," said Aslan. "For the fruit always works – it must work – but it does not work happily for any who pluck it at their own will. If any Narnian, unbidden, had stolen an apple and planted it here to protect Narnia, it would have protected Narnia. But it would have done so by making Narnia into another strong and cruel empire like Charn, not the kindly land I mean it to be. And the Witch tempted you to do another thing, my son, did she not?"

"Yes, Aslan. She wanted me to take an apple home to Mother."

"Understand, then, that it would have healed her; but not to your joy or hers. The day would have come when both you and she would have looked back and said it would have been better to die in that illness."

And Digory could say nothing, for tears choked him and he gave up all hopes of saving his Mother's life; but at the same time he knew that the Lion knew what would have happened, and that there might be things more terrible even than losing someone you love by death. But now Aslan was speaking again, almost in a whisper:

"That is what *would* have happened, child, with a stolen apple. It is not what will happen now. What I give you now will bring joy. It will not, in your world, give endless life, but it will heal. Go. Pluck her an apple from the Tree."

For a second Digory could hardly understand. It was as if the whole world had turned inside out and upside down. And then, like someone in a dream, he was walking across to the Tree, and the King and Queen were cheering him and all the creatures were cheering too. He plucked the apple and put it in his pocket. Then he came back to Aslan.

"Please," he said, "may we go home now?" He had forgotten to say "Thank you", but he meant it, and Aslan understood.

CHAPTER FIFTEEN

THE END OF THIS STORY AND THE BEGINNING OF ALL THE OTHERS

"You need no rings when I am with you," said the voice of Aslan. The children blinked and looked about them. They were once more in the Wood between the Worlds; Uncle Andrew lay on the grass, still asleep; Aslan stood beside them.

"Come," said Aslan, "it is time that you went back. But there are two things to see to first; a warning, and a command. Look here, children."

They looked and saw a little hollow in the grass, with a grassy bottom, warm and dry.

"When you were last here," said Aslan, "that hollow was a pool, and when you jumped into it you came to the world where a dying sun shone over the ruins of Charn. There is no pool now. That world is ended, as if it had never been. Let the race of Adam and Eve take warning."

"Yes, Aslan," said both the children. But Polly added, "But we're not quite as bad as that world, are we, Aslan?"

"Not yet, Daughter of Eve," he said. "Not yet. But you are growing more like it. It is not certain that some wicked one of your race will not find out a secret as evil as the Deplorable Word and use it to destroy all living things. And soon, very soon, before you are an old man and an old woman, great nations in your world will be ruled by tyrants who care no more for joy and justice and mercy than the Empress Jadis. Let your world beware. That is the warning. Now for the command. As soon as you can, take from this Uncle of yours his magic rings and bury them so that no one can use them again."

Both the children were looking up into the Lion's face as he spoke these words. And all at once (they never knew exactly how it happened) the face seemed to be a sea of tossing gold in which they were floating, and such a sweetness and power rolled about them and over them and entered them that they felt they had never really been happy or wise or good, or even alive and awake, before. And the memory of that moment stayed with them always, so that as long as they both lived, if ever they were sad or afraid or angry, the thought of all that golden goodness, and the feeling that it was still there, quite close, just round some corner or just behind some door, would come back and make them sure, deep down inside, that all was well. Next minute all three of them (Uncle Andrew now awake) came tumbling into the noise, heat, and hot smells of London.

They were on the pavement outside the Ketterleys' front door, and except that the Witch, the Horse, and the Cabby were gone, everything was exactly as they had left it. There was the lamp-post, with one arm missing; there was the wreck of the hansom cab; and there was the crowd. Everyone was still talking and people were kneeling beside the damaged policeman, saying things like, "He's coming round" or "How do you feel now, old chap?" or "The Ambulance will be here in a jiffy."

"Great Scott!" thought Digory, "I believe the whole adventure's taken no time at all."

Most people were wildly looking round for Jadis and the horse. No one took any notice of the children for no one had seen them go or noticed them coming back. As for Uncle Andrew, what between the state of his clothes and the honey on his face, he could not have been recognized by anyone. Fortunately the front door of the house was open and the housemaid was standing in the doorway staring at the fun (what a day that girl was having!) so the children had no difficulty in bustling Uncle Andrew indoors before anyone asked any questions.

He raced up the stairs before them and at first they were very afraid he was heading for his attic and meant to hide his remaining magic rings. But they needn't have bothered. What he was thinking about was the bottle in his wardrobe, and he disappeared at once into his bedroom and locked the door. When he came out again (which was not for a long time) he was in his dressing-gown and made straight for the bathroom.

"Can you get the other rings, Poll?" said Digory. "I want to go to Mother."

"Right. See you later," said Polly and clattered up the attic stairs.

Then Digory took a minute to get his breath, and then went softly into his Mother's room. And there she lay, as he had seen her lie so many other times, propped up on the pillows, with a thin, pale face that would make you cry to look at. Digory took the Apple of Life out of his pocket.

And just as the Witch Jadis had looked different when you saw her in our world instead of in her own, so the fruit of that mountain garden looked different too. There were of course all sorts of coloured things in the bedroom; the coloured counterpane on the bed, the wallpaper, the sunlight from the window, and Mother's pretty, pale blue dressing jacket. But the moment Digory took the Apple out of his pocket, all those things seemed to have scarcely any colour at all. Every one of them, even the sunlight, looked faded and dingy. The brightness of the Apple threw strange lights on the ceiling. Nothing else was worth looking at: you couldn't look at anything else. And the smell of the Apple of Youth was as if there was a window in the room that opened on Heaven.

"Oh, darling, how lovely," said Digory's Mother.

"You will eat it, won't you? Please," said Digory.

"I don't know what the Doctor would say," she answered. "But really – I almost feel as if I could."

He peeled it and cut it up and gave it to her piece by piece. And no sooner had she finished it than she smiled and her head sank back on the pillow and she was asleep: a real, natural, gentle sleep, without any of those nasty drugs, which was, as Digory knew, the thing in the whole world that she wanted most. And he was sure now that her face looked a little different. He bent down and kissed her very softly and stole out of the room with a beating heart; taking the core of the apple with him. For the rest of that day, whenever he looked at the things about him, and saw how ordinary and unmagical they were, he hardly dared to hope; but when he remembered the face of Aslan he did hope.

That evening he buried the core of the Apple in the back garden.

Next morning when the Doctor made his usual visit, Digory leaned over the banisters to listen. He heard the Doctor come out with Aunt Letty and say:

"Miss Ketterley, this is the most extraordinary case I have known in my whole medical career. It is – it is like a miracle. I wouldn't tell the little boy anything at present; we don't want to raise any false hopes. But in my opinion –" then his voice became too low to hear.

That afternoon he went down the garden and whistled their agreed secret signal for Polly (she hadn't been able to get back the day before).

"What luck?" said Polly, looking over the wall. "I mean, about your Mother?"

"I think – I *think* it is going to be alright," said Digory. "But if you don't mind I'd really rather not talk about it yet. What about the rings?"

"I've got them all," said Polly. "Look, it's alright, I'm wearing gloves. Let's bury them."

"Yes, let's. I've marked the place where I buried the core of the Apple yesterday."

Then Polly came over the wall and they went together to the place. But, as it turned out, Digory need not have marked the place. Something was already coming up. It was not growing so that you could see it grow as the new trees had done in Narnia; but it was already well above ground. They got a trowel and buried all the magic rings, including their own ones, in a circle round it.

About a week after this it was quite certain that Digory's Mother was getting better. About a fortnight later she was able to sit out in the garden. And a month later that whole house had become a different place. Aunt Letty did everything that Mother liked; windows were opened, frowsy curtains were drawn back to brighten up the rooms, there were new flowers everywhere, and nicer things to eat, and the old piano was tuned and Mother took up her singing again, and had such games with Digory and Polly that Aunt Letty would say "I declare, Mabel, you're the biggest baby of the three."

When things go wrong, you'll find they usually go on getting worse for some time; but when things once start going right they often go on getting better and better. After about six weeks of this lovely life there came a long letter from Father in India, which had wonderful news in it. Old Great-Uncle Kirke had died and this meant, apparently, that Father was now very rich. He was going to retire and come home from India forever and ever. And the great big house in the country, which Digory had heard of all his life and never seen would now be their home; the big house with the suits of armour, the stables, the kennels, the river, the park, the hot-houses, the vineries, the woods, and the mountains behind it. So that Digory felt just as sure as you that they were all going to live happily ever after. But perhaps you would like to know just one or two things more.

Polly and Digory were always great friends and she came nearly every holidays to stay with them at their beautiful house in the country; and that was where she learned to ride and swim and milk and bake and climb.

In Narnia the Beasts lived in great peace and joy and neither the Witch nor any other enemy came to trouble that pleasant land for many hundred years. King Frank and Queen Helen and their children lived happily in Narnia and their second son became King of Archenland. The boys married nymphs and the girls married wood-gods and river-gods. The lamp-post which the Witch had planted (without knowing it) shone day and night in the Narnian forest, so that the place where it grew came to be called Lantern Waste; and when, many years later, another child from our world got into Narnia, on a snowy night, she found the light still burning. And that adventure was, in a way, connected with the ones I have just been telling you.

It was like this. The tree which sprang from the Apple that Digory planted in the back garden, lived and grew into a fine tree. Growing in the soil of our world, far out of the sound of Aslan's voice and far from the young air of Narnia, it did not bear apples that would revive a dying woman as Digory's Mother had been revived, though it did bear apples more beautiful than any others in England, and they were extremely good for you, though not fully magical. But inside itself, in the very sap of it, the tree (so to speak) never forgot that other tree in Narnia to which it belonged. Sometimes it would move mysteriously when there was no wind blowing: I think that when this happened there were high winds in Narnia and the English tree quivered because, at that moment, the Narnia tree was rocking and swaying in a strong south-western gale. However, that might be, it was proved later that there was still magic in its wood. For when Digory was quite middle-aged (and he was a famous learned man, a Professor, and a great traveller by that time) and the Ketterleys' old house belonged to him, there was a great storm all over the south of England which blew the tree down. He couldn't bear to have it simply chopped up for firewood, so he had part of the timber made into a wardrobe, which he put in his big house in the country. And though he himself did not discover the magic properties of that wardrobe, someone else did. That was the beginning of all the comings and goings between Narnia and our world, which you can read of in other books.

When Digory and his people went to live in the big country house, they took Uncle Andrew to live with them; for Digory's Father said, "We must try to keep the old fellow out of mischief, and it isn't fair that poor Letty should have him always on her hands." Uncle Andrew never tried any Magic again as long as he lived. He had learned his lesson, and in his old age he became a nicer and less selfish old man than he had ever been before. But he always liked to get visitors alone in the billiard-room and tell them stories about a mysterious lady, a foreign royalty, with whom he had driven about London. "A devilish temper she had," he would say. "But she was a dem fine woman, sir, a dem fine woman."

The Chronicles of Narnia
by C. S. Lewis

C. S. Lewis's wit and wisdom, his blend of excitement and adventure with fantasy, have made this magnificent series beloved of many generations of readers. The final book, *The Last Battle*, won the Carnegie Medal for 1956.

Each of the seven titles is a complete story in itself, but all take place in the magical land of Narnia. Guided by the noble Lion Aslan, the children learn that evil and treachery can only be overcome by courage, loyalty and great sacrifice.

The titles, in suggested reading order, are as follows:

The Magician's Nephew
The Lion, the Witch and the Wardrobe
The Horse and His Boy
Prince Caspian
The Voyage of the Dawn Treader
The Silver Chair
The Last Battle

Order Form

To order books direct from the publishers, just make a list of the titles you want and send it with your name and address to:

Dept 6,
HarperCollins Publishers Ltd,
Westerhill Road,
Bishopbriggs,
Glasgow G64 2QT

Please enclose a cheque or postal order to the value of the cover price, plus:

UK and BFPO: Add £1 for the first book, and 25p per copy for each additional book ordered.

Overseas and Eire: Add £2.95 service charge. Books will be sent by surface mail, but quotes for airmail despatch will be given on request.

A 24-hour telephone ordering service is available to Visa and Access card holders on 0141-772 2281.